MURDER IN THE BAND ROOM

Ann Grieves Mysteries

By PATRICIA SNELLING

Published in New Zealand by Patricia Snelling

Contact: patricia.snelling.books@gmail.com
Website: patriciasnelling.com

This is a work of fiction. Any resemblance to
actual persons, living or dead, or actual events
is purely coincidental and not to be construed
as real.
Scripture quotations are taken from the Holy
Bible, New International Version® NIV®
Copyright © 1973, 1978, 1984 by International
Bible Society. Used by permission of
Zondervan. All rights reserved worldwide.

A catalogue record for this book is available
from the National Library of New Zealand

Martin Joyce – Cover Designer
Judith Little – Editing Support

****

Other Books by Author:

Missing On Lion Rock
When Hope Went South
Jessie's High Country Heart
Mack The Good Shepherd
Missing On Kawau
Unshakable (Peacehaven Series)
Broken Web (Peacehaven Series)
Rescue Net
Louis's Garden Party (Preschool book)

****

Website: patriciasnelling.com

****

Disclaimer

This novel is written in British English with
New Zealand colloquialisms or Kiwi slang

Chapter One

Calamity Ann—that's what they called her when she was working in the police force—pensioned off at fifty with enough money to buy a seaside cottage in Cockle Cove. Constable Ann Grieves was her name when she first started working for the West City District Police until she lived up to her name by weeping over every dead body she encountered. That's when her colleagues began calling her Calamity Ann instead of Grieves to distract her from the crying—and it worked!

After a year of rearranging her flower garden, making preserves for older people in the neighbourhood and walking her beloved Beagle dog, Scout along the boulevard each day, she was ready to abandon the quiet life and take on another calamity in her capacity as a private investigator.

Scout was an ex-police dog gifted to her by a colleague, after being retired from drug-sniffing at the airport. He was a splendid companion, especially since her husband, Terry was killed in a drug bust shootout two years earlier.

Ann's close friend, Martha had invited her to stay on her small rural holding in Riverlea to help solve the suspicious shenanigans going on in the local brass band—the Riverlea Brassholes. The musicians usually met on a Wednesday from 1 pm to 4 pm and consisted mainly of retired players and those who were self-employed or on shift work and could get the time off during the day. But now they were preparing to compete in the provincial Brass Band Contest against several other rural bands, and they had stepped up their rehearsals to a Monday, Wednesday and Friday. It was an annual event, and this year it was going to held at the end of the month at their band hall—but there were complications. Martha said she'd rather wait to elaborate when they get together, as it was a sensitive issue, best not discussed over the phone.

♫ ♫ ♫

Ann's 1979 Land Rover had almost given up the ghost she'd thought until her friendly neighbourhood mechanic said it could still keep driving another hundred-thousand kilometres. Packed to the hilt, she was ready for a lengthy stay with her lifetime friend, Martha. They were once esteemed cornet players in the Highbrass East band—especially Ann, who was a virtuoso. When she quickly moved up the ranks from Detective Constable to Detective Inspector, the police department transferred her to Southland, and that put an end to her band days.

Retiring in her early fifties, she couldn't wait to move north again where it was warmer and purchased a seaside cottage in Cockle Cove. Her trustworthy, Besson cornet remained a prized possession.

Whenever she felt like stirring her deathly quiet neighbourhood, she would take the instrument out for a blow, which would drive the aged residents out for their daily walk.

The drive through the countryside invigorated her as she inhaled the sweet smell of freshly cut hay through her open window. Arriving in Martha's driveway, she swerved to avoid squashing her pink, miniature Kunekune pig, Hyacinth who was like a child to her.

Martha rushed outside to greet her. 'Sorry, Ann—she will jolly well get in the way. It's just curiosity, as she loves people,' she said, as Ann hauled herself out of the vehicle while Scout whined his disapproval. The two women hugged.

'As long as she gets on with Scout. You said she doesn't mind dogs, and he is very gentle, even with the cat next door,' said Ann, hoping Scout wouldn't let her down.

'It would be too difficult for me to leave him behind, as I don't know anyone in the neighbourhood who would come to my home each day to walk and feed him.'

'Don't worry—he'll be fine. Perhaps just keep him on a lead to start with.'

'Thanks, I think so too.'

Ann hauled her suitcase out of the vehicle and left Scout there while she dragged it up the steps.

'Let me show you to your room,' said Martha, taking her friend's laptop bag and scurrying along the hallway to the guest room.

'Here you are—I've already made your bed up, and there is a fresh towel and flannel on the bedside table for you.'

'Oh, it's gorgeous, Martha. What a lovely room—all coordinated with spring flowers,' Ann said, glancing at the bedcover and curtains.

'Why don't you sort your things out and join me for afternoon tea after you've attended to Scout, and then I'll go over the reason I brought you here—which is of some urgency. Use the wardrobe at leisure.'

Martha hurried away while Ann hastily unpacked, mindful Scout sat waiting for her in the car.

Hyacinth hadn't budged. The pig sat next to Ann's vehicle as though she waited for Scout to join her—or at least that's what Ann hoped was the case. She clipped the lead on the dog and held him close, expecting him to make a commotion with the pig in his space, but he quietly sniffed her all over, while the pig gave strange grunts and squeals. *Thank the Lord— they will be friends.* Ann led him through the gate around to the backyard and tied him to the veranda.

'Oh, there you are. Here's a bowl you can use for Scout. You can fill it from the hose at the side of the house. Let me,' said Martha, fussing over her.

When they had both attended to Scout, Martha took Ann inside for a welcome afternoon tea—fresh

scones with home-made strawberry jam and cream. It
took Ann no time at all to feel at home.

Chapter Two

'It's so good of you to come here, Ann. I couldn't have coped with this much longer—I'm at my wit's end,' said Martha stammering, as she passed Ann another scone.

'What's going on—I mean you didn't say over the phone. You just said something about some shenanigans at the band room.'

'Goodness! Did I not say? I can't remember our conversation now. I had the most terrible fright the night before I rang you.'

Ann took a bite of her scone and then placed it back on the plate. 'What on earth happened?'

'Somebody locked me in the music library on Friday afternoon when I was alone sorting out the music for the contest.'

'Yeeks, that sounds ominous.'

'I agree—I spent the entire night in that tiny, stuffy room on the floor. There wasn't even a chair in there—only the step ladder for reaching the top shelves. Luckily, a few boys from the Junior Band turned up for a rehearsal the next morning, and the key was still in the lock. They heard pounding on the door and let me out just in time as I rushed to the bathroom.'

'You sure it wasn't the adolescent boys who locked you in?'

'I'm sure. They are respectful kids whom I've known for years—Frank used to teach them music. Anyway–they weren't there on Friday.'

'It's a strange thing to happen,' said Ann.

'One of my neighbours said they saw my car in the band room carpark late that night on passing. She guessed I was busy sorting music but didn't think to check to make sure.'

'I'd have thought she would have investigated when she saw no other cars parked outside and should have known you wouldn't have been in the band room late at night on your own.'

'I agree,' said Martha. I suppose it's partly my fault for not locking the door straight away after everyone had left, but I thought the last person out would have flicked the snip on the door before leaving.'

'Why were you sorting music on Friday, anyway?' asked Ann.

'That's because, when we shifted it from the old band room, all the folders got muddled up, and I'm now sorting it into alphabetical order. That's besides attempting to find music for Andre our conductor, known by our members as AC—since he introduced a new piece for the concert section for the contest. I have to sort and photocopy the sheets for each player, and it's so much work!'

'So, it could have been someone who knew you would be there—perhaps a prankster unless you know of anyone who would have a grudge against you.'

'No, I don't know anyone who would want to do that. I'm pretty shaken up and still trying to get my head around it. I also need to finish getting the music organised for our next practice tomorrow, because we'll be rehearsing three afternoons a week until the contest. Will you help me with the music sheets in the morning?'

'I'll do more than that—I'll find the culprit who pulled that stunt. It is probably someone from the Junior Band.'

Martha poured them both a second cup of tea.

'No, it's not them. It's something more sinister than that—I'm sure someone did it with malicious intent. They are trying to sabotage our participation in the contest.'

'You think so? Why would anyone want to do that?'

'They don't want us to get the cup. We're going head to head for the prestigious Sylvester silver cup title against Haversham Hooters. They held the title for decades until last year when our band won by a few points, and it devastated them.'

'You think one of them has come all the way here to stalk the band and do you harm? How would they have got in without a key? That is not a reason to lock you in the music library.'

'The key was still in the door—unless it were one of our players who knew I would be in the library that evening.'

'It could just be someone with a personal vendetta against the band,' said Ann. 'We have to be sure about what we're dealing with, and we don't have any clues yet.'

'I tell you what. Let me help you get the music sorted tomorrow, and once we've done that, I want you to note down every incident in the band room that you think has been suspect during the last month and from now on. I can come along to your band practices and help you with your role in the kitchen and sort music. That way, I'll get to observe what's happening myself.'

Martha burst into tears. It had all been too much for her, but now her friend had come to her rescue. She couldn't have asked for a more qualified person than Ann who could see it would be a massive wrench for Martha to let go of her when the time came for her to return home, but for now, she would make the most of having her stay. First, they required a well-needed catch-up before getting into the nitty-gritty of the unusual happenings in the band room.

They wandered out the back into the garden and sat on the old walnut bench seat Martha's late husband had built her.

'So—why do they call Andre AC?'

'Oh, that makes it easy on us. His full name is French—Andre Chauvin, and when he joined the band, most people couldn't pronounce it properly, and we ended up calling him AC. He didn't seem to mind.'

'That makes sense.' Ann ran her fingers along the smooth wood on the bench. 'This is gorgeous.'

She saw the anguish in Martha's face and gently touched her friend's arm. 'How long is it now since Frank passed away? You must miss him—I know how close you were.'

That brought another snivel to Martha who took out a starched, white handkerchief and blew her nose.

'Four years now, but as long as I continue to do his work in the music library, he'll still be with us in spirit, as we always sorted the music together.'

'What happened to the old hall they used as a band room? I heard there had been a fire?'

'It was totally damaged, but the music was still intact in the library—would you believe? Must have been a miracle. The firemen think it was arsonists. We were all gutted when that happened.'

'Where are you holding rehearsals now?'

'In a disused packing shed donated to us by Tom Sidwell, the farmer who lives at the end of

Appleyard Road. It has all we want—bathroom facilities, kitchen and sufficient seating for a sizeable group. The committee did a grand job of renovating the shed that already had two offices. They erected shelves in one for a music library, while Andre and the band secretary use the other for administration. The packing shed already had two change rooms—a separate one for men and women.'

'Good old Tom—sounds like a honey.'

'He used to operate a mixed orchid before he retired. The trees are still there, and he gives us bags of fruit now and then—whatever is in season. The Black Doris plums are delicious. Since his wife died, he loves listening to the bands day or night he can hear from his house.'

'Oh, look at those two. They've become bosom buddies,' said Ann, glancing at Scout and Hyacinth nuzzling each other.

Martha chuckled. 'I think it'll be safe for them to run around the backyard together. It's big enough, and it looks like they want to get to know each other better.'

'Sure—I'll let Scout off his lead,' said Ann, walking over to do the honours of introducing the pig to Scout. In no time at all after a few more sniffs, the animals shadowed each other as they trotted off barging through the hens.

'Great! I can relax knowing Hyacinth will entertain him while I'm here,' said Ann. 'Now let's get down to brass tacks and discuss how we'll get this music sorted for tomorrow. How far have you got?'

Martha eagerly spoke at length about how far she was with arranging the music into each instrument section and what they were to do next.

'If we put in a few hours in the morning before the band arrives, we should make quick work of it,' said Ann. 'If you don't mind, I'd like to attend all the rehearsals with you between now and the contest. I need to note any subterfuge amongst the ranks and find out whether any your players could have locked you in.'

'Absolutely. I need your help, as I said—not only with the music but in the kitchen. I feel better already.'

Martha indulged Ann for the rest of the day ushering her around her extensive garden, giving a running commentary of the botanical classification of every tree and flower she had planted.

'I've got a chicken roast ready to go in the oven and some of my home-made raspberry and rhubarb wine to wash it down. It's low alcohol too, so entirely healthy,' said Martha, winking at Ann who picked a lavender flower head and squeezed it in her hand, sniffing the aromatic scent.

'It will be good having a catch-up after such a long time,' she replied.

Chapter Three

The Bottom of the Problem

After they had finished sorting out the music before practice, Martha gave Ann a guided tour of the sizeable band room that the owner had used as a fruit packing shed, which the Riverlea Brassholes had renovated as a custom-built band room. Martha impressed Ann by pointing out the unique features of the building.

'That's our instrument room there, and on your right, the admin office shared by Andre and Lyall, the band secretary, and we ladies even have our own changing room!'

'Well, I'm impressed,' said Ann. 'This is a significant improvement since you and I both played with Highbrass East.'

'I know—old Tom has spoiled us. He subdivided this piece of land, so it is all belongs to us. He lives just over the fence there,' she said, pointing out the window to a farmhouse sitting behind a clump of bare apple trees.

'What's behind the black curtains?' asked Ann. 'That looks interesting.'

Martha laughed. 'Oh, you must take a look. That's the highlight of this entire building.'

Martha hurried to the front of the building and drew the curtains. 'Voila!' she cried. 'Here is where we will hold our provincial contest.'

Ann's mouth dropped wide open as her eyes came out on stalks. 'Unbelievable—your own stage! This is the best band room I've ever seen—and amongst an old orchard at that!'

The women made their way back to the kitchen in readiness for the onslaught of players who would expect a cup of tea before practice.

'Thanks for all your help this morning, Ann. I wouldn't have done it without you,' Martha said, patting her on the back.

'A problem shared is a problem halved,' said Ann, with a broad smile.'

'Let's put the urn on for some tea. I've got some chicken sandwiches from last night's roast, and we can have a quick lunch before practice begins. I brought enough milk for us, and whoever is on the milk roster this month will be here soon.'

'Splendid idea—I'm dying for a drink,' Ann said, flicking the switch. 'Once you are playing, I'll sit on the side-line and listen. Just tell the conductor I'm staying with you and we used to play in the same band years ago. Let him know I'm not interested in taking banding up again.'

'Don't worry—I'll make sure they won't try to railroad you into anything.'

'Just for now, it's best not to let on that I'm a private investigator. We want to catch whoever it is red-handed if it's one of your players.'

During the tea break at half-time, Martha introduced her friend to some of the curious band members. AC, the conductor, immediately asked Ann to bring her instrument to next practice. Before she could answer, Martha whisked her away back into the kitchen.

'I must get to the bathroom before we play again,' said Martha. They busied themselves, clearing away the cups from the servery ready to load them into the dishwasher. Ann almost dropped a stack of them as a mighty bellow burst forth from the direction of the bathroom. The two women shot off to investigate, and there was poor Will, a trombone player writhing around on the floor like a cut snake with his trousers half off. His face was bright red as he tried hard to restrain himself from screaming.

Martha bent over him. 'What is it—what's happened? Shall we call the ambulance?'

He had hold of his posterior and burbled something that Ann, standing by, didn't quite catch as he gasped for breath, almost choking.

Martha looked up at her. 'I think he said burning—the toilet seat is burning.'

'It's okay, Will, I'm a retired nurse,' said Martha. 'Tell me where it hurts.'

Will grabbed his backside again. 'It must be the toilet sanitiser—it's burning my skin. Someone has doused the seat with it during our break.'

'Wait—let me look,' said Ann, who had years of experience sniffing chemicals during forensic investigations.

After sniffing the toilet seat, she looked inside the bathroom pulling out a bottle of pure ammonia. She removed the lid and instantly recoiled, clapping her hand over her nose and mouth. 'This isn't toilet sanitiser—it's ammonia! No wonder you screamed— it's not for cleaning toilet seats! Quickly—close the door and rinse your skin off in the hand basin,' said Ann.

By this time, half the band stood in the hallway observing the drama.

'Wait—I'll warn everyone,' said Martha.

'There are two toilets, and this one is out of bounds until we sort it,' she cried. 'We'd better remove the ammonia while there's a lunatic in our midst. Most people only use it to wash the floors. There's disinfectant in the cupboard, so why didn't they use that?'

Within a quick time, Will stumbled out of the band room with one hand holding his rear end and his other arm draped over the shoulder of Len, the drummer. They shuffled out to Len's station wagon where the victim lay sprawled out on his stomach on the back seat while on their way to the nearest doctor.

Ann still didn't let on to the musicians she was there to investigate whether there was a criminal at large. Someone had locked Martha in the library, and it was no accident. No one would be stupid enough to do that unwittingly, and Ann was determined to get to the bottom of it.

Chapter Four

Because of the incident in the bathroom with the trombone player, the first afternoon of the contest rehearsals had turned out to be a complete disaster. The villain had succeeded. The two women arrived home exhausted, and Martha's nerves were in a worse state than before.

'Come on—you have a nice hot bath after that fiasco while I rustle up a meal,' said Ann. 'I brought plenty of groceries with me from home and one of the steak and kidney pies you like. I have a bar of chocolate for afters.'

'You're a darling—I don't think I could take much more of this. I don't know how you could do your detective job—I'd be useless.'

'I suppose you've got to be cut out for it. My father was also a top-ranking detective, remember?'

'I sure do, and you've certainly followed in his footsteps, dear old Ted, rest his soul.'

The women sat up late drinking hot chocolate and sharing comical anecdotes from their past band days.

'I'm still wondering how anyone could have known that Will would use the bathroom at that precise time. How would they have been able to swap the liquid over just before he walked in?' asked Martha, rejuvenated after the hot chocolate drink Ann had made her with full milk.

'Ah no—I don't think the offender is specifically targeting any one member. Their goal is to take out the whole band, possibly to prevent you all from participating in the contest, unless you can think of another reason.'

'No, I can't. That's a good enough reason—mark my words.'

'Therefore, anyone of you could have been the victim of the ammonia attack.'

'That's creepy—I wonder who'll be next. We have to warn the players they are all targets,' said Martha, curling up on the couch hugging her knees.

'No, Martha—don't say a thing. If the felon is in your midst and a wolf in sheep's clothing, we don't want them to know they're under surveillance. I need to observe what transpires between now and the contest. Please leave it to me.'

'Right you are, Detective Inspector,' said Martha with a warm smile.

'One thing I'd like you to do. It would be wise to get the band room's lock changed tomorrow, just in case someone had got in with a key. Would you be able to arrange that with the caretaker?'

'I think so—I'll phone Bob first thing in the morning.'

'I'd like to help you while I'm here. You've got enough on your plate with the contest and all this unpleasantness. How about letting me fix up your garden out the front? Would you mind if I buy some flower plants and put them in the bed by the steps? That'll cheer you up.'

'Oh, Ann, that's kind of you—I've let things slip since Frank passed. This contest takes up much of my time at present, and I'd love to see some blooms in the garden.'

'Good, I'll go to the garden centre in the village tomorrow morning.'

♬ ♬ ♬

After Martha's phone calls to Andre and Bob the caretaker, she enjoyed pottering around at home while Ann ran errands for her in the village.

Bob arranged for the locksmith to meet him at the band room at midday, who changed the lock and gave Bob three keys—one for himself, Martha and Andre and handed Bob the bill to give to the band's treasurer. Bob told Martha he would cut a key for Matt the Junior Band conductor. That meant there were only four people with the key.

Ann enjoyed the drive into the village with Scout on the back seat, passing all the orchards and small farm blocks and breathing in the clean air. It was reminiscent of her childhood, growing up in the country.

She heard an unusual grunt and then she got the whiff of a putrid stench. Guessing the odour emanated from a silage store outside in a field, she closed her window.

The grunting continued. 'What's going on, Scout—are you making those noises—what's up, buddy?'

Pulling into the shoulder of the road, she turned to check out Scout and gaped with her mouth open wide at the sight of a pink pig wallowing in its muck on the back seat. Instantly Scout hurtled onto the front seat to get away from her.

'Hyacinth! What do you think you're doing in here?'

She didn't need to ask, as it was apparent. Ann couldn't understand why Martha called her Hyacinth, as she was far from looking like a beautiful flower. But the pig was relaxed about it all—in fact, Ann was sure she caught a glimpse of a smug look on her face. Now she would have to turn around and take the animal home to get the Land Rover cleaned up, and then if she still had the motivation, head back to the village again.

Martha was embarrassed about the disgraceful performance her beloved pet had displayed and took her out back to clean her up. 'Shame on you!' she bellowed, as Hyacinth looked away. 'Sorry, Ann, it's the first time she has done anything like that. She must have been excited.'

'No worries,' said Ann, as she scrubbed the back seat using a pile of rags Martha had given her. After spraying the car with an air freshener, the unpleasant smell still lingered.

She drove back to the village, chuckling all the way and thinking what a far cry her life was now from her days of working in the force living on the edge. She wasn't sure which one she would prefer, and this episode had put paid to any romantic notions of embracing small farm animals as pets.

That afternoon, after hours of weeding and composting the bed in the front garden, Ann filled the plot with brightly coloured petunias, snapdragons and daisies. Emotional Martha wept when she saw what Ann had done for her, as the blooms were a welcome reprieve from the mayhem at the band room.

♫ ♫ ♫

Ann sat in her bedroom, mulling over the first two suspicious incidents with the Riverlea Brassholes.

The day of the chemical attack, she had furtively watched the behaviour and body language of each band member before and during their tea breaks, carefully noting every detail in her black notebook. But it just didn't seem workable that a musician would go to such extremes to create havoc. It must have been an ex-band member who still held a key, as it's an easy feat to get another key cut.

The entire thing made little sense. Ann would have to attend every rehearsal between now and the contest to familiarise herself with each player and find out if any of them had a motive to harm the band.

'Are you there, Ann?' called Martha from outside the bedroom door. 'Dinner's ready—I'm about to dish up.'

'On my way!' Ann called.

The women sat enjoying the chicken and thyme pie Martha had prepared and chatted about the events of the last few days.

'Tomorrow I must print off copies of music for the absent players in preparation for the rest of the rehearsals.'

'I'm looking forward to seeing if anything else happens now that you've had the lock changed,' said Ann.

'Well, we'll soon find out. Bob will distribute the keys today—Andre and myself. I doubt if either of those men is a suspect.'

Chapter Five

A Tireless Foray

The atmosphere in the band room felt as though one could cut the air with a knife since the chemical attack, and things weren't the same for Martha since the night she'd spent in the library. She needed to keep looking over her shoulder and scan every musician.

As soon as the pair arrived for the rehearsal on Wednesday, Martha got to work collating the music they'd sorted ready to hand to the players while Ann went to the kitchen and to turn on the urn and began getting out the cups. When Martha had finished in the library, the two women sat and ate the sandwiches they'd brought with them.

'I'm dying for a cup of tea with my food, but there's no milk in the fridge,' said Ann.

'There's a weekly milk roster just while we have stepped up the practices this month before the contest.' Martha stood and scanned the list on the wall next to the servery. 'It's Winnie this week. She usually gets here early so we should have time for a drink before we play.'

It didn't take long before the band members started traipsing in with their instruments and setting up, and the usual ones came to the kitchen leaning over the servery waiting for their tea. It was common for some of them to have a cup before they started and then again at the half-time break. There were the moaners who complained if it wasn't on time, or if the servers didn't put out the right biscuits, as most of them went straight for the chocolate sorts.

'Hey, there's no milk again. Who's bringing it—aren't they here yet?' ranted Victor, a euphonium player.

Ann looked up from delving in the cupboard for the sugar. 'I think Martha said Winnie Whistleblower is on the roster this week. She must be running late,' said Ann sheepishly, offended that the ignorant man didn't even greet her with a *hello* before ranting about his cup of tea.

'Well, we always seem to run out. Couldn't the woman have asked someone else to get it?'

Ann felt her cheeks burn as her blood boiled.

'Listen here—if it's so important for you to get a cup of tea before you play, perhaps you could get in your car and rush up to the dairy along the road, or you could even bring your own,' she said calmly, with a half-smile.

'Is that right? Humph!' he said and stalked off.

'Oh, don't take any notice of him,' said Martha grimacing. He's always sounding off, and well done for putting him in his place—it'll do him good. There is usually enough milk in the fridge during the week as we get a large bottle, but sometimes the Junior Band who use the building on Saturdays and Tuesdays forget to get their own and use ours.

Ann rattled her car keys. 'Would you like me to pop up to the dairy and get some?'

'No—I'll ask Bob to get it if Winnie doesn't turn up. I've just seen him arrive in the car park.'

When everyone sat with their instruments ready to play, Martha received a text on her cell phone. She discreetly checked it and then raised her hand in the air.

'What is it, Martha—we're about to start?' Andre growled, his eyebrows snapping together.

'A message from Winnie. She's still at home, and a vandal has slashed all four tyres on her Ute. It's their only vehicle, so she won't be at practice unless someone can collect her.'

'Really? That's terrible. She lives out in the backwoods so that will hold us up,' Andre said, with a displeased tone.

'I'll go, said Ann from the sideline. I'm not playing, so it won't matter if I'm gone. If Martha could give me her address and warn her—I'll go now.'

Martha dashed over to Ann who stood at the door.

'I'll be as fast as I can. Perhaps I can investigate the situation while I'm at it,' whispered Ann, as the women stood behind the open door.

'This'll be another one to record in your black book,' said Martha. 'Winnie is our top flugelhorn player and wins her solos every time she plays at contests. We can't lose her.'

'I'm on my way—we'll swap notes later.' Ann grabbed her bag and shot off as the band played Phantom of the Opera.

♫ ♫ ♫

Although Martha had given Ann complete instructions on how to get there, she had taken two wrongs turnings ending in dead-end country lanes. Without a GPS in her Land Rover, she struggled to follow the map on her phone. Finally guided by instinct and an astute memory of the directions Martha had given her, she found the driveway leading to Winnie's farmhouse.

'Oh, thank God you could come,' said Winnie as she rushed up to Ann who tentatively stepped out of her vehicle, dreading stepping on pig dung. She too had Kunekune pigs as well as a menagerie of other farm animals.

'I would hate to let the band down, but this is ruthless,' wailed Winnie, as Ann took her in her arms.

'Don't you worry—we'll get to the bottom of this—believe me, we will,' said Ann.

She walked over to investigate Winnie's Ute, and her face dropped as her eyes scanned the remains of the slashed tyres—slithers of rubber scattered on the ground.

'That was vicious. Someone has sure got it in for you,' said Ann. *I can bet it's the same mongrel who committed the offences in the band room, but I won't tell Winnie that.*

'Joe, my husband is down at the Police Station right now making a statement. I guess they'll be around to check it out later.'

'Okay. For now, let's get you to rehearsal. You're a vital player in the contest—and we need the milk,' she said, chuckling.

Winnie's chatter and remonstrations about the moral state of the universe could not drown out Ann's constant rumination of the attack on the players. She didn't know the members that well and had to fast track a way of getting to know them individually, which would call for some intrusion on her part. Before they arrived at the band room, Ann enlightened Winnie about the attacks, leaving her perplexed and unbelieving that a band member was capable of such malicious actions.

Ann had saved the day by transporting the traumatised woman to her practice milk—and all. When they arrived, Ann put the complaining euphonium player in his place when she sidled up to him at half-break and muttered in his ear, 'No point crying over spilt milk, is there!' walking off triumphant.

♫ ♫ ♫

Ann prided herself in that she had good relations with the local police at Cockle Cove, and since she'd been living there had aided them in solving several cases in and around her home since her so-called retirement.

The band committee had been reluctant to report the first two suspicious incidents to the police, as a few of the more opinionated players had deemed both events as accidental. But Ann would not rest her case and knew there was much more than *accident* involved.

The following day, a vehicle arrived in Martha's driveway at midday while Ann was busy throwing bread to the flock of birds that frequented Martha's garden. It was Winnie, racing through the gate waving a document at her.

'I've got the police report. They came around yesterday and conducted a thorough search of the property. They discovered that the intruder had cut the wire fence behind the house after arriving on foot. It must have been while Joe and I were down the back of the farm feeding the horses before lunch.'

'That's brilliant news—I mean that they know that much. And I see you've got your new tyres already. I guess your vehicle insurance will cover that.'

'I think so—Joe is handling that side of things.'

Martha joined the women. 'Hi, Winnie. Good to see your Ute is back on the road. Any news?'

'Hi, Martha.' Winnie rattled off the police report to her. 'The police said there had been a spate of break-ins and burglaries in our area recently, so they think it could be connected.'

'I'm not sure they are. Did you tell them about the series of incidences that occurred in the band room recently?' asked Ann.

'No, I didn't think I should say anything yet. I'd rather wait and see what the rest of the band want to do about it.'

'Mmm ... I think they have been misled somehow, but we'll wait and see,' said Ann grimacing.

'Join us for lunch, Winnie.' said Martha

'Thank you, but I'd better get on. Joe has the blacksmith coming this afternoon, and I said I'd give him a hand to bring the horses in.'

'We'll see you tomorrow afternoon at rehearsal then,' Martha replied.

'Yep, see you then. Let's hope there are no more repercussions of the past week. It's enough to put one off and stay home.'

Ann grasped Winnie's shoulders.

'No way, Winnie. If there is a guilty party in the band room, they have won by coercing you to give up—that's their whole aim. You've got to fight, as I think we have a battle on our hands. Although the contest is at stake, you are also at risk of losing the band altogether.' Ann glanced at Martha, seeking her approval.

'She's right, Winnie. I believe our band is under attack—someone wants to drive us out-of-town.'

Winnie's mouth dropped open, and her cheerful, bubbly disposition changed. Walking towards her vehicle with a long face, she turned towards the two women.

'Don't worry—you can count on me. I won't give up.'

Chapter Six

One Man's Meat is Another Man's Poison!

'I used to love Fridays,' said Ann, licking the marmalade off her fingers and buttering another piece of toast. 'Like all detectives, I used to go hard out all week living on the edge, and when Friday night came, I'd collapse in a heap with a glass of whisky and sleep the rest of the weekend. That's when the booze got the better of me, and I started getting stomach ulcers which forced me on the wagon.'

Martha poured them both a mug of coffee.

'How did you relax after you eliminated the whisky from your life? That must have been difficult.'

'Not really. I've got God in my life like you, and since the day I made that decision, I haven't looked back. I occasionally indulge in a glass of Guinness if I'm particularly uptight, but that's okay, the doctor says.'

'I don't mind if you do that here. I'm not against alcohol in moderation, so feel free.'

'Thanks, Martha. I'm wondering what dodgy delights await us this afternoon. Did I tell you I've started scrutinising each band member quizzing them one by one about their backgrounds and keeping a dossier on them all?'

'No, you didn't. How far have you got?'

'Not far. I only have time to do it when I'm not in the kitchen after band practice when some of the players are drinking at the bar or sitting around chatting.'

'I can't wait to see what you come up with when you've finished. Don't worry about mucking around in the kitchen with me—it's not that difficult with a dishwasher. You concentrate on subtly interrogating my colleagues.'

'We'll see how we go. I might manage both,' said Ann winking. 'Would you like me to feed the hens this morning? I can do that before I walk Scout.'

'Yes, please. That'll give me time to give my cornet a clean before practice. I've been going to do it all week.'

After they cleared up the dishes, Ann went to the garden shed to find the pellets for the hens. She scooped them into a bucket and scattered them around the yard. Martha had already collected the eggs, so that was enough for the morning.

She went back to the house and took the dog's lead from the hook at the back door.

'I'm off for a walk with Scout.'

'Right you are. See you back here soon,' Martha replied.

Ann searched around the garden for Scout, calling his name. It was an extensive property covered in trees and shrubs, and Scout loved to go exploring. He must be up the back of the section, she thought.

As she scanned the fence line towards the rear, Ann spotted a piece of steak lying on the ground next to the fence. It looked fresh as though it hadn't been there long. Just as she'd caught sight of it, so did Scout and he raced across the field heading directly for the meat. Like a real Beagle detection dog, he gave a yelp, sniffed at it and sat next to the beef wagging his tail.

'Good boy, well done.' Ann pulled a treat from her pocket, which Scout whipped from her hand.

She felt terrible, removing the meat before the dog's eyes, but this was suspect. The ex-police dog had not lost his touch. She hurried into the house and took a pair of disposable rubber gloves from her bedroom before racing back outside to scoop up the meat. She went back inside, waving the beef in front of Martha, before placing the evidence inside a plastic sandwich bag.

'What's that? I thought you'd gone out for your walk?' Martha said, wiping her hands on her apron.

'You didn't throw a piece of raw steak out in the backyard for Scout by the Camelia trees, did you?'

'That's a strange question to ask. Why on earth would I do that? Meat is too expensive to be throwing it away, even for a beloved dog.'

'Someone threw this over the fence, and I scooped it up off the ground. According to Scout, it's suspect.'

'That's so weird,' said Martha, screwing up her face. 'Why do you think someone has done that?'

Ann frowned, her eyes narrowing. 'I think they drugged or worse—poisoned it. I guess they intended to harm Scout.'

'Oh, no. You mean we're now under attack here at my home. What are you going to do—I mean, how can you be sure?'

'I need to get the meat tested. Do you know of any vets around here?'

'Yes, of course—there's Riverlea Vet just up in the village behind the Fruit Shop.'

'I'll head off there now, so I can be back in time for us to go to band practice.'

'We'll have to be on guard outside now. I hope they don't harm my animals. It's as though they want to drive us all out of town, not just away from the contest. That's sick,' Martha said with a quaver in her voice.

'You're right. We're dealing with an unbalanced, obsessed character for sure.'

Martha began wringing her hands. 'If the test shows that someone drugged the beef, we must report it to the police.'

'I know we will, for sure. I'll get off now. You'd better keep an eye out while I'm gone. I'll take Scout with me.'

Ann didn't feel like attending the rehearsal that afternoon after she dropped the meat off to the vet for testing. He said he'd send the sample to the laboratory and wouldn't have the results until after the weekend. It was far too long to wait, and she was desperate to find out if the culprit had laced the meat with poison—then it would become a police matter. What upset her most was the thought of finding her dear canine companion dead all because of a stupid trophy! But if she let herself wilt, she would let Martha down and unbeknown to them, the rest of the band.

At the band room, Ann detected an air of melancholy amongst players arriving through the front door. Perhaps seeing Will writhing in agony from the horrendous chemical attack had upset them too.

'No Will today? I thought he would have recovered by now,' Ann said to one of his fellow trombone players busy setting up his music stand.

'He won't be here today—in fact, he hasn't been able to sit down since the incident. It burnt the skin right off his backside—completely raw it is. He can't lie on it, poor beggar.'

Ann stood aghast. 'Well, that's dreadful news. Thank God he didn't get it in his eyes. That stuff is lethal.'

She dashed over to Martha, who was filling the urn. 'Poor Will's out of action. That's one down. Whoever it is, tried to take you and Winnie out, but at least you're both still in the race. I wonder who'll be next.'

'Shush—Terrence on second horn is eavesdropping, and he doesn't miss a trick,' Martha whispered.

'Terrence—tea is not ready yet. Give us some space!' she snapped.

The horn player trundled off and plonked himself back on his seat then started sorting his music with a long face.

'I hope Will recovers before the contest. At least he can practice at home standing upright,' said Martha. They both tried hard to contain their merriment.

It had been a tough week for the band, and Ann knew they should not rest on their laurels, as she was sure there was more to come.

Although they played the contest pieces right through, the band seemed to have lost its lustre, she thought, as though a black cloud had descended over the group. Perhaps they weren't in denial as much as she'd assumed, they were.

They'd come through the afternoon unscathed, but there had been four absences at that rehearsal. Perhaps that could have been the reason there had been no skulduggery, as the culprit may have been one of the absentees.

♫ ♫ ♫

After a welcome meal cooked by Martha, Ann took Scout for an extended walk, scrutinising every person on the pavement who passed her. Since the incident with the meat, her daily outings with Scout were no more the pleasant, relaxing strolls she once enjoyed. Now she felt the need to continually look over her shoulder, eyeballing with suspicion anyone who glanced at her.

That evening after a late supper, Ann grilled Martha about the four players who had not turned up for the rehearsal.

'No, Ann. There's not one of them I could label as enemy material. They are all men and women of upright character.'

Ann stood next to Martha in the kitchen, stirring hot milk with a wooden spoon ready to pour into the mugs of chocolate powder. This was an evening ritual that they had discovered was akin to them both.

38

Martha opened a kitchen cupboard. 'Look what I've got to cheer us up—some of those Ginger Kisses you like. Come on, let's relax in the lounge.'

Ann quizzed Martha about each band member one by one, noting every detail in her black book which was her daybook.

They appeared to be ordinary people with uneventful lives. If there was a traitor amongst them, the women were one step ahead of them.

'I'm expecting the results of lab tests tomorrow morning. The post gets delivered in Riverlea on a Saturday, doesn't it?' asked Ann, gathering up their mugs.

'Yep, it comes usually around ten or thereabouts. I'm getting nervous about that. I hope it's not what you said it could be. What was the name of that drug you mentioned to me the other day?'

'*Acepro*—it's a sedative and dangerous stuff for dogs in the wrong hands,' said Ann, with a fragile voice.

Martha stroked her arm. 'Don't worry, Ann. Have faith that it will all work out.'

'I guess you're right. If the culprit had wanted to kill Scout, they would have used a lethal dose, which they didn't.' Ann wrapped her arms around herself. Only God knew that when she was on the streets as a top-ranking detective, she had been as sharp, and severe as any of the men, but she had a soft heart— especially for helpless innocent people and animals.

'I think I'll turn in now, Martha. See you in the morning.'

♫ ♫ ♫

Ann woke late on Saturday morning with the piercing sunlight bursting forth through the gap in the drapes. She tried to turn over and go back to sleep, but Martha's rooster took it upon itself to stand on the shed outside her bedroom and start crowing.

'Darn silly fowl,' mumbled Ann. 'No wonder Martha calls you *Rowdy.*'

She pulled the cover over her head, but it was no good. Although she'd been awake half the night mulling over the recent attacks on the band, she would not get back to sleep now.

Sluggishly she pulled on her dressing gown and trudged into the kitchen to see Martha who was already up as perky as ever.

'Goodness! I hope you don't mind if I say, but you look ghastly. Are you okay—you're looking peaky?'

'I'm alright—just didn't get much sleep last night. It's like the old days when I was on a case, and it dragged on. I just couldn't get my mind off that piece of meat thrown in the garden. It has to be a ruthless person who would take such risks.'

'Here, get this into you. I've made some toast if you'd like some. Wait until you get the results of the test and we'll take it from there. I'll take Scout for a walk today if you like.'

'Thanks for the offer, Martha, but I thought you might like to come for a ride out to Hobsonville Point with me and Scout. There's a pleasant coastal walkway out there and a cute café with great food—my shout.'

'Sounds like a splendid idea. I've got to feed the geese and chickens first and tidy up the house.'

'I'll give you a hand.'

'Wait, I think I heard the postie's van—I'll look,' said Martha, retying her dressing gown and trundling outside.

Within minutes she was back inside.

'It's here—it looks like it's from the lab,' spouted Martha with wide eyes.

Ann suddenly became animated as she took the envelope and tore it open. While her eyes scanned the document, Martha was bursting to read it. 'What does it say,' she blurted.

Ann's face dropped as she shook her head and froze in her chair.

'Ann! Tell me, is it bad news?' Martha pleaded.

'I'm afraid so. It's just as I suspected. They laced the meat with that anaesthetic agent called *Acepro*. The vet is under obligation to report it to the police, as it's a controlled drug.'

'Wow, this is getting serious,' Martha cried.

'I gave the vet the go-ahead, and I said I'd talk to the police.'

'Are you going to tell them the malicious episodes at the band room could be linked to Winnie's attack?'

'I'm not sure. We are the ones most likely to catch the culprit, as we are on the inside. The police won't have sufficient evidence. We have no proof of your incident in the library and the same as the injury to Will. They'll say they were both accidental, and the fact that no one owned up about using ammonia to clean the toilet seat is not evidence of a malicious attack. The police will put that down to the guilty party being too embarrassed to come forward after unwittingly using the wrong cleaning fluid. It's all circumstantial evidence.'

Martha placed a rack with toast on the table along with her home-made lemon curd. 'Would you like to have muesli first? Or I've got other cereals.'

'No thanks, Martha. Please don't fuss—I'm not that hungry right now. A bit of toast will do. Who knows? Maybe I'll work up an appetite when we're walking along the coastal walkway.'

'So, I guess we must see what else transpires next week. I'm scared. Who knows what that person can do after trying to kill poor Scout?'

Ann paled suddenly. 'No, they weren't trying to kill him—just scare us. The vet said the concentration of the drug was just the dose they would use to sedate a dog before surgery. It would have put him in a deep sleep long enough to put the wind up me.'

'Well, the whole incident has rocked me!'

'Come on, Martha. Let's finish breakfast and get these chores done, so we can get out the door and blow out the cobwebs. I think we should not think or talk about it for the rest of the weekend.'

Chapter Seven

A Spanner in the Works

It was the second week of rehearsals, and Ann spotted that Will was still not at band practice on Monday afternoon, as she glanced around the hall before the afternoon session was about to start.

'The poor man. Who would have thought one could visit the bathroom and end up in that state,' she hissed at a player who handed her his empty coffee mug.

He leaned over and murmured, 'Glad it was him and not me, unfortunate fellow,' he said, hurrying over to his seat.

Andre stood on his podium, ready to make an announcement. 'Now—quiet everyone. There are a few things I need to bring to your attention. We have four players away today, so you will have to do your best without them.'

He went into essential details about the lock being changed and how in the old band room in past years several band members possessed keys. He enlightened the band that Martha, Bob and Matt will be the only ones with keys, apart from himself, to minimise the security risk.

During Andre's announcement, he mentioned nothing about Will, Winnie and Martha's serious incidents, as Ann had cautioned Martha not to breathe a word to Andre or anyone that they suspected foul play. If the culprit was a band member, they wanted to make sure he or she did not have an inkling they were under surveillance.

'Now—I have made some changes to our concert piece, *Glenn Miller Medley* and have asked Martha to print those off for you. You can cross out the sections we won't be using—please don't do so on an original copy.'

Martha stood over the copier disgruntled. Someone had turned it off, and now she had to wait until it warmed up and rebooted. Andre started the band playing a hymn to give Martha time to get the music ready.

'Jolly machine!' she ranted to herself. 'Every time I need to print something off in a hurry, this happens!' She caught herself when the music stopped, as she was in hearing distance from the band.

She rebooted the machine twice to no avail. All it did was grunt and cough and then stalled after she pushed the copy button.

Furtively she shuffled out the door and stood within view of a horn player sitting on the end of the row, discreetly waving at him to come. He got up and joined her in the library.

'Sorry to disturb you, Jim, but I need help,' she muttered. 'The copier's jammed, and there doesn't seem to be paper caught in there.'

Jim leaned over the machine and opened it up. 'Can you get me a torch? There used to be one in this room somewhere,' he mumbled.

Martha extracted a small LED torch from a drawer nearby and handed it to him.

After a succession of grunts and groans from Jim as he huffed and puffed, pushing and pulling at the mechanism inside the oversized copier, he stood up waving an object. 'Here's the offender,' he said, holding up a medium-sized shiny spanner. 'I'm afraid it has wrecked the copier. You must arrange a technician to repair it, and it will cost a packet to get it fixed.'

'What? How on earth would that have got in there?' Martha fumed.

'I don't know—but mind if I get back to my seat?' Jim patted her on the back and left her standing in a quandary.

Andre called out to her, 'Martha—I don't think we can wait much longer for that music. What's the holdup?'

'I'm sorry, Andre. Jim and I have found a problem. An object we found jammed inside the copier machine has damaged it, and we'll be without one until it's repaired.'

The band went quiet. Martha sensed the unsettling tension.

'We must get a tech out here to repair it,' said Martha.'

'Goodness! What else could go wrong? This contest hasn't exactly been plain sailing,' Andre muttered to the band, mopping his brow with his handkerchief.

'I've got a large laser copier at my office and can do that photocopying for you. I'll take it home and do it', said one of the trombone players.

'Let's stop for a tea break, band,' said Andre. 'You've done well this afternoon, and when you are back in your seats, I want you to run through all the contest pieces, except for the *Glenn Miller Medley* which hopefully we'll have back by Wednesday.'

Martha and Ann couldn't wait to swap notes, but first Ann made a play for a few people she had marked in her notebook as unknown entities, especially those who had come from another city to join the band.

After their break, Andre called for the band's attention before they started playing.

'Don't forget we are having a dress rehearsal this Saturday here at the band room, and I want you all in full uniform. Thanks to Bob, who wears two hats and is not only our revered caretaker but also our expert video operator—we will film the entire session. Report here on time at 10 am, and we'll start playing and recording at 11 am. Seeing I'm dragging you out on a Saturday and you'll be playing most of the day, the committee will supply pizzas for lunch.'

'Hey—will that include a glass of beer?' Pete, from the horn section, asked.

Andre shot daggers at him, ignoring his remark.

As the band were about to play, some of them pulled out their phones and notebooks to jot down the details for the dress rehearsal.

Driving home from practice, Ann took the doglegs in the road cautiously in the pouring rain. It was challenging to focus on the slippery highway while Martha constantly spouted her theories about the spanner turning up in the copier's body.

'I think we can eliminate Jim from trying to sabotage the copier. Andre said that Matt, the Junior Band conductor used the copier on Saturday afternoon, and no one was in the building on Sunday.'

When they arrived inside the house, there was a message on the answerphone for Ann from Detective Sergeant Isaac Yule asking if he could visit the next morning and would she phone to confirm a time.

Chapter Eight

DS Isaac Yule was right on time the next morning, as he rapped on the front door prompting Scout to cause a commotion barking.

Ann opened the door as the dog slobbered all over him. 'Cut that out, boy!'

'Come in. Sorry about that—he'll lick you half to death if I let him. Get outside, Scout!' She grasped his collar and pulled him through the hallway out the back door closing it behind her.

'Come into the lounge and sit yourself down. I'll see where my friend, Martha, is.'

Ann met her down the hallway. 'Come and join us, I need moral support—please!'

'I don't know how I can be of much help. We're still not going to report the other malicious incidents, are we?'

'No, not yet. You and I need to do some more investigations into that. We can report it anytime. Let's just deal with the attack on Scout. It's too close to home to leave that one.'

As the women joined Isaac in the lounge, he was still looking at the band trophies and photos on the wall and turned around to introduce himself.

'Detective Sergeant Isaac Yule–you can call me Isaac.'

After shaking their hands, Isaac shot a glance at Martha's photos.

'These are yours, aren't they? Is this your family holding their instruments?'

Martha blushed. 'That's right—all four of them played in bands since they were at primary school.'

'I recognised you in the family photo,' he said, taking a genuine interest.

'Frank, my late husband used to teach all the young ones who joined the band. Now—take a seat. Can I make you a cup of tea or coffee?'

Isaac gave her a warm smile. 'No, thanks. I'm running out of time, as there's been a serious incident in town that I need to follow up. Let's get down to brass tacks.'

He looked at Ann. 'You're the lady who phoned me about the dog poisoning? Can you let me see the lab report?'

Isaac perused the document and photographed it on his iPhone. 'Can you tell me exactly what happened?'

Ann found it difficult to leave out the events leading to the attack on Scout, as it was pertinent to the case, but she was determined to solve that enigma her way. She only wanted to use Isaac to build a case to get police security around Martha's home and rattled off a summary with variations.

Isaac shook his head. 'Well, if you don't know of anyone who has significant animosity towards you or who hates your dog—it is an enigma. People don't randomly try to kill people's animals.'

Ann gave Martha a wry smile. 'The dog is mine—Scout is his name, and he hasn't been here long. I've only been with Martha for a week, and he doesn't bark and annoy the neighbours.'

'I see you have a small menagerie on your property, Martha which I could see over the fence while I was standing at your door.'

'Oh yes, they're my family. Silly of me really, but my adult children live all around the country, so the animals are a substitute.'

'I want to suggest you get cameras put around your house for added security. Do you have a cell phone?'

Martha pulled her phone out of her jacket pocket. 'Yes, I have this one. My children got together and bought it for my birthday.'

Isaac leaned over to inspect it and raised his eyebrows. 'Goodness me. That's one of the latest iPhones.'

'Yes, it is. They know I love taking photographs and this phone has an excellent camera.'

'Getting back to your home security. Do you have anyone who could install CCTV cameras around your house?'

Martha frowned and started wringing her hands. 'One of my sons is an electronic technician, and he installed alarm cameras around his own home. Perhaps I could ask him. He's the only one of my children living in Auckland.'

'Splendid idea! That will give you peace of mind about your animals too,' said Ann, rubbing Martha's arm.

'The hardware store sells plaques you can fasten to your fence warning people that say—*Warning! CCTV camera alarms in operation.*'

'That sounds wonderful,' said Martha, perking up suddenly. 'I'll ring my son, Louis today and get it organised.'

'And I'll start making enquiries in the village to investigate whether anyone has noted any other dubious activity going on in the area.'

Isaac pulled out a notebook and began writing. 'There is something else I wanted to tell you. That drug, *Acepro,* is a controlled drug that only vets can access. It will be worth forensics trying to trace who dispensed that drug in this part of the woods. Perhaps someone stole it, but we need to find out.'

'That's a point. Perhaps it's a retired vet or even a vet's nurse who got hold of it. Do you know of any, Martha?' Ann asked.

Martha stared at the floor, shaking her head. 'No, I don't think so, but I'll sleep on it. Maybe something will spark my memory.'

'Well, I must be off. I'll get in touch after I've completed the follow-up with the drug. Please let me know if you receive any further harassment.'

Martha and Ann thanked him and saw him out to his vehicle. They both felt more relaxed, knowing they had someone else on board to help them solve the puzzle.

Martha put the kettle on and made them both a cup of tea which they had at the dining table.

'I'll bet you were chafing at the bit to tell Isaac you're a retired Detective Inspector,' said Martha, with a chuckle.

'You're right—it was difficult to restrain myself,' Ann replied. 'But it would have ruined it for us. We just need to keep to our plan until we see this thing through. I can always tell him further down the track. Often the Force doesn't look kindly on amateur sleuths, but one could hardly call me that. I have assisted the Force with investigations in my village recently. It's a wonder DS Yule hasn't heard of me.'

I'll give my son, Louis, a call and organise those cameras and then I can relax.'

'I remember Louis when he was at kindergarten. I'd love to see him.'

'You're going back a long way now, Ann. We were only in our twenties when we played in the

Highbrass East band, and then I married Frank not long after I met you.'

'We've got some history together, that's for sure.'

'I'm off to phone Louis now.'

Chapter Nine

Ann didn't leave Martha's side at the Wednesday practice. She had her super-scan eyes on, making sure she missed nothing.

Andre leaned over the servery to chat with Ann while Martha served the tea.

'I don't think I've thanked you for helping Martha with the music—and in the kitchen. It has taken the pressure off us all.'

'It's no trouble—I'm delighted to be amongst fellow bandsmen and women, and I'm plugging for you to win this cup.'

'Hmm, I detect a smidgen of nostalgia, do I not?'

Ann grinned, assuming his effort at subtle manipulation, got her interested in joining them.

He smirked and walked away to circulate with the others.

Martha joined Ann to help finish cleaning up the cups that players had brought into the kitchen.

'I just spoke to two guys on the trombone section. Did you notice poor Will is still away?'

'No, I didn't, but I would have expected him to be back by now,' replied Ann.

'Apparently, he's miserable—poor bloke. The ammonia burnt the skin right off his backside!'

Ann tried to contain herself as she imagined that spectacle. The two women looked at each other and burst into laughter, trying to pull themselves together as more players entered the kitchen with their cups.

'We'd better get this lot tidied up,' said Martha, with a wide grin on her face.

There were three players absent for this practice, and Ann thought it uncanny that for the rest of the afternoon, there were no suspicious incidents. Did that mean that the villain was one of those who didn't turn up that day? Ann jotted down the names of absentees, with Martha's help. She discussed her suspicions about the missing players with Martha as she drove back to Riverlea.

'Perhaps we should concentrate on this lot as a shortlist,' said Ann. 'I want to go over their profiles with you again.'

♫ ♫ ♫

To Martha's delight, her son, Louis arrived the next morning with the CCTV camera alarm system and installed it by midday. He'd even purchased the metal plaques with alarm alert warnings and fastened them to the fence. Martha indulged him in a light lunch after he demonstrated the use of the iPhone app. Before driving off, Louis invited his mother and Ann to a barbeque at his home on the upcoming Sunday—the day after the dress rehearsal for the contest.

'Goodness—that was a flying visit,' said Ann, after he'd driven off. 'He sounds busy.'

'I guess he is raced off his feet—that's why I rarely ask him to come out here to do anything. He has a young family and barely gets time to spend with them while running his own business.'

'Where does he live—do you have far to go to visit him?'

'On the other side of Auckland out Botany way.'

'Wow, that's far away. I understand he would find it difficult to visit often.'

'Yes, it is, but I miss my grandchildren. They come and stay with me occasionally, but I doubt whether that will happen while that nutter is roaming around. I didn't let on to him about the attack on Scout, as I will never see my grandchildren if I tell him. Even then, I won't bring them here while the perpetrator is still at bay.'

'I've got some lovely, bright petunias to put in that garden bed by the front steps,' said Ann, trying to lighten Martha's mood. 'That will lift our spirits.'

Martha gave her a warm smile. 'You're a darling—you always were a comforting soul. Do you mind if I shoot off and do some practice? I'm playing a duet with Errol—*Pie Jesu* it's called.'

'Really? That's a beautiful composition—one of my favourites. I used to play the soprano part at concerts.'

Martha's expression changed. She came alive suddenly. 'Please ... come with me and have a blow. I'd love that. I've got a spare soprano cornet—it was my Frank's. It's much easier to practice a duet with another person.'

'Oh, I'm not sure I'll be up to scratch these days. Though, I see what you mean.'

She glanced at the face that resembled that of an eager child and gave in. 'Oh, alright—you win. You know how I like to blow my own trumpet,' she said with a chuckle.'

'Thanks so —I appreciate it.'

Taking a break from the intense situation of the pandemonium at the band room, playing a duet with Martha lifted her spirit.

A tuneful harmony emanated from the open upstairs window—the spare room which Martha used as a music room. Hyacinth and Scout froze as if mesmerised when *Pie Jesu* resonated into the garden below.

When they finished playing, Martha stood gaping at Ann with a beaming smile.

'You haven't lost a beat! That was wonderful. You're a real waste not being part of a band anymore.'

'Well, I always keep up my practice, but I have other things I like to do too, and I enjoy my free time when I'm not sleuthing.'

'Thanks so much, anyway. I feel better about our dress rehearsal tomorrow. We're all set now.'

Martha picked up her iPhone. 'Hey, check this out.' They both laughed watching the app for CCTV displaying her backyard with the animals. There was her pet goose, Snow Flake herding Hyacinth and Scout as though she was a sheepdog. They took off around the side of the house, and the women could see everything on camera.

'That rascal goose. I don't know what to do with her. She's not like other geese and does this with the hens too. I think she's just bored,' said overgrown with blackberry.' Martha. 'There's also Petticoat, my nanny goat who competes with Snow Flake bossing everyone around. But she's usually down the back of my little orchard where it is

'Isn't it marvellous that you can press a button on your iPhone and watch what's going on around your property. This is a fine example.'

'Yes, for sure. To be honest, I don't know if I would have been able to relax without them. I was getting edgy.'

'We're halfway there—don't even think about giving up now,' said Ann. 'I promise we'll find the felon. Eventually, they'll trip themselves up.'

'We've just got to make it to the contest and win that jolly cup, and hopefully, all the skulduggery will stop.'

'Mmm,' said Ann. 'The only thing is there'll still be a criminal at large, and if they are a member of the band, they will always be a threat. If we don't find them, you'll always have that hanging over you, contest or not.'

'Oh, dear, I suppose you're right. It doesn't bear thinking about,' mumbled Martha, reverting to her previous downcast state before they had played the duet together.

Ann could see the strain in Martha's face. Deep furrows formed in her brow and crow's feet etched in the corners of her eyes revealed nights of broken sleep. Ann would have to work smarter to catch their attacker.

That night, she too burnt the midnight oil—her mind racing, rehashing the events that occurred during the last two weeks. She would have to identify persons of interest and create thorough personal profiles of all twenty players individually. First, if it were someone from the band, she could eliminate the four people who had keys—Martha, Bob, Matt and Andre. Those people were sacrosanct. Then there was Winnie, and Will who were both victims, so that cancelled them out. The day Will suffered the chemical attack, three players were away, so she could exclude them from her investigations, which left twenty to probe.

I'll have my work cut out, that's for sure, she mused, as she drifted off to sleep, sitting up in bed still in her dressing gown.

Chapter Ten

A Sticky Situation

The mood of the band always heightened whenever they were at a dress rehearsal for a contest. Bob arrived early to open up, and Martha and Ann were not far behind.

As some of the players' partners arrived, they got to it right away—arranging the stage, setting up chairs and stands while one of them managed the lighting.

A bandsman's partner offered to help prepare the food for the luncheon break.

'I'll cut the pizzas up when we heat them later—just leave it to me,' said May.

The musicians arrived in their uniforms and were ready to play by 10.30 am. The only one who hadn't turned up for the rehearsal was Errol, the soprano player scheduled to play the duet with Martha.

'What am I going to do, Andre? There's no sign of him in the car park, and he's not answering his cell phone,' said Martha.

'I don't know. I can't wait for him any longer as the sound tech has arrived to do the audio recording, and Bob only handles the camera. We pay him, and it's not cheap. Jolly nuisance Errol not letting us know.'

Martha grimaced. She wondered what else could go wrong.

'Wait—what about your friend, Ann? I heard she is quite a virtuoso on the soprano—or at least she used to be. Perhaps she might bail us out just for today until we get hold of Errol.'

'That's a superb idea!' Martha replied excitedly.

'Why don't you trot over and ask her while I find Chad to see if he can sort out a soprano cornet for her. Surely she won't turn us down.'

Martha found Ann placing her muffins onto plates in the kitchen.

'You don't have to do that—several partners are offering to give a hand with the food.'

'I get fidgety just sitting around. I want something to do.'

'That's why I came to get you. We desperately need your help, and Andre sent me to beg. Errol, my duet partner, hasn't turned up, and no one has heard from him. Andre asked if you'd give *Pie Jesu* a try. I didn't tell him you accompanied me yesterday and played brilliantly. Surprise him!'

'Goodness! You've caught me on the hop. I don't have a uniform, and I'll appear out of place in the group photo.'

'We have plenty of women's uniforms hanging in the change room, and I'm sure there's one in your average size. Come—let's look.'

While Ann was trying on a uniform with Martha's help, Chad, the instrument custodian chose a shiny soprano cornet from the instrument room and gave it to Andre.

Within a short time, Ann came out appearing like a bandswoman and bumped into Andre who was standing on tenterhooks outside the ladies' change room holding the cornet for Ann.

'Thank you so much. You are rescuing us from a right pickle. Don't worry if you're rusty.'

Ann glanced at Martha, who beamed at her.

The band got off to an awkward start, and to top it off it there was more trouble to come when they played the *Glenn Miller Medley*.

'What's happening with you, Len? You're supposed to be using your hi-hat cymbals for this piece. Are you half asleep?' Andre glared at him.

'Someone has rigged them—I mean they sabotaged my drum set. They've put superglue between the cymbals and punched a hole with a tool in my bass drum. How did that happen?'

'Maybe it's time we called the police. This is getting out of hand,' said Andre, trudging over to look.

'I'll just make do, but the effect won't be the same, so I must get it repaired before the contest.'

'Thanks, Len. If you wouldn't mind just improvising to get through this rehearsal and I'll discuss it with you after we finish.'

The whole band had a baffled expression on their faces, and it was disturbing for them all Ann realised. She gave it everything she could to make up for the distressing incident.

Ann tugged on Martha's sleeve. 'Come on, Martha—our turn. Let's show them what we can do and play to save the band.'

The women stood at the front of the stage and gave the best performance the band had heard, of *Pie Jesu* with their accompaniment. Ann astounded them producing soprano notes as clear as a bell, while the musicians almost stopped playing, mesmerised.

Andre walked over to the two women. 'Well done, that was an excellent performance—both of you.'

He turned to Ann and shook her hand. 'You saved the day, and I don't know how to thank you.'

Following the rehearsal, Andre received a phone call from Errol. 'Sorry, Andre, I'm at the hospital with my wife. She fell down the front steps this morning and broke her ankle, and I left my phone in the car.'

Ann caught the end of the conversation— Andre telling him how she'd saved his bacon.

♫ ♫ ♫

When they had finished eating a well-earned, late lunch, Ann overheard Andre discussing the attack on the drum kit and elbowed Martha to listen in too.

'I checked with the drummer from the Junior Band who said there was no problem with the drum kit at Saturday's practice,' said Len, his face reddening with anger.

'You can call Bob to arrange for the police to come and investigate.'

'Andre—I had a similar incident happen when someone locked me in the music library. I think instead of calling the police we could ask the Junior Band if they know if anyone has been playing pranks on our lot. They are here twice a week on Tuesday evenings and Saturdays. It's possible,' said Martha.

'Jolly brats, a few of those boys are. There are one or two who stretch the limit. I'll talk to Matt, their conductor and ask him if he has had anything of that nature occur.'

'I think that would be better. We don't want to recriminate the young ones. They just need a proper caution from Matt that he'll throw them out of the band. Perhaps it's a troubled child.'

'All right then, I'm suitably convinced. But I must help organise someone to repair this drum kit.

Sorry about all this, Len, but we'll get it sorted before long.'

Chapter Eleven

Most of the time, Ann and Martha took turns driving their vehicles to the band practices seeing they were more frequent than usual, and after the rehearsal, Ann drove her Land Rover and pulled into a car park in Riverlea Village.

'Have you got anything out for dinner?' she asked Martha.

'No, but I would love takeaways tonight. The fish shop is next to the butcher over there in the corner. Let's look.'

The seductive aroma of fish and chips wafted onto the pavement as they followed their noses to the shop.

'Let me get them, please, Ann. It's the least I can do after all you've done to help me these last two weeks.'

'Are you sure?'

'Absolutely—what will you have?'

After discussing their meal orders, Ann waited outside. A tap on her shoulder startled her, as she turned around to see DS Yule standing there.

'Sorry, Ann—I didn't mean to alarm you. Martha told me about the new surveillance cameras. How is it going—anything suspicious?'

Oh, hello, Isaac. 'No—only Martha's goose, Snow Flake bullying my dog and her pet pig.'

Isaac laughed. 'That would be a sight to behold. I was about to drop by and give you feedback about police enquiries we've made around the village.'

'How did you get on?'

Isaac lowered his voice. 'There have been no criminal activities in the area recently, and no one appeared to have seen anything suspicious that day. It must have been someone who wanted to scare you both, as the dose of the drug in the meat wasn't lethal.'

'I suppose we have to work out why they want to frighten us,' said Ann, secretly knowing precisely what the motive was.

'Let me know if there's anything else I can do to help and call me if you have any concerns.'

He put his head in the shop's door and waved at Martha before he continued along the footpath to the carpark.

Martha arrived carrying boxes with their orders.

'Mmm, that smells good,' said Ann. Let's get home to eat it before it gets cold. Don't forget we're going to Louis's barbeque tomorrow. I'll take the meat and sausages out of the freezer tonight.'

♫ ♫ ♫

It had been an exhausting day both mentally and physically, and they decided to have an early night. Or at least that's what Ann thought she would do until her head hit the pillow and her brain wouldn't stop running through the names of players she had eliminated from her list of suspects.

How and when anyone could have tampered with the drum kit with so many players hanging about?

It was no good—no matter how exhausted she was since the dress rehearsal and Len's sticky foray, she dived into her jacket pocket for her black book.

Picking up her pen from the bedside table, she sat back in bed, resting her head on the headboard.

She perused the long list of names and profiles of each player with additional details of interest. At the back of the book, she kept a record of band members eliminated from her possible suspect list—this information she transferred into a dossier so she could later compile a report.

So far, along with Martha, Bob and Winnie, there was Andre, Will and the three players who were away the day of the ammonia attack. When someone sabotaged the copier, there were four people away, and Jim helped Martha fix it, so she could eliminate him, most likely. As she scanned through the list of names, she placed a tick beside each of their names.

'Oh, I'd better add Errol to the file too—and Len. That makes fourteen I can tentatively put aside for now,' she muttered, placing a tick beside their names.

She was about to put her book away then hesitated. 'Hmm—I've forgotten about Jim who discovered the offending object jammed in the copier.' She pondered momentarily. *Matt said that the copier was working fine at Junior Band, and no one used the hall on Sunday, the day before that incident.*

This method seems to work, so long as it's the same person committing all these acts of sabotage, but at least it can be a shortlist, she thought, slipping her notebook into her bedside drawers, plumping up her pillows and turning out the light.

♫ ♫ ♫

Ann enjoyed the barbeque, watching Martha's pre-school grandchildren entertaining everyone on the lawn. As she had no children of her own, this pulled at her heartstrings, as she seldom saw her young nieces and nephews who lived in Australia but spending time with Martha's kin made her feel part of their family.

Driving home from Botany, Martha discerned from Ann's quiet mood, that she was deep in thought until her Beetle Volkswagen turned off the motorway onto the country road and ran into a pothole, shaking her back to reality.

'You're still with us then?' Martha chuckled.

'Oh—sorry, I was miles away. I'm constantly trying to work out what motive would cause a band member to go to such extremes to damage your band. Think carefully, Martha. Is there anyone amongst you who might have a score to settle within your ranks?'

Martha mulled it over as she continued to drive on the back road out to Riverlea through the countryside.

'No, not as far as I know. Unless someone has an issue that I'm unaware of that they've kept to themselves. To be perfectly honest, if anything is going down in the band, I'm usually the first to hear, as I've been there the longest.'

'I think it has to be someone within the band—that's my stance, but it is pure conjecture at this stage through my process of elimination.'

'I just hope that person isn't so unbalanced to become violent. Apart from Will and his burnt backside, the other incidents have been more prankish. But what extremes will the culprit go to? It seems they haven't finished yet.'

'It sounds as though somebody bears a huge grudge, but we'll get to the bottom of it. Whoever it is doesn't miss a trick and makes sure they carry out their dastardly deeds when players are preoccupied, or the victim is alone. Just as you were when you sorted music alone that evening and you had assumed the last person out of the band room would have snipped the lock that afternoon.'

'That is so scary now you say it like that. To think someone came back to the hall and crept in while I was inside the library. They could have done worse. I have always felt safe there until now.'

'Thank God they didn't harm you, but you will have to take precautions from now on as we don't know what extreme lengths they will go to.'

'I'm so glad you're with me on this. I think it would have forced me out of the band if I had to deal with it on my own,' Martha said glumly.

'Buck up—the contest is in two weeks, and Riverlea Brassholes will win, no matter what. So, don't give up now, Martha. Where's your faith? If it is someone in the band trying to sabotage the contest, then at least it will soon be over,' said Ann, hoping that what she was saying was right as they arrived in Martha's driveway.

Chapter Twelve

Andre had given the band a day off from practice on the Monday following the dress rehearsal. They had excelled at their performance which was captured on video, and Andre had sent a copy to everyone by email.

Martha pointed at her computer screen. 'Look at this, Ann—you're famous.' I'll forward it to you.'

Ann leaned over her shoulder and flashed a beaming smile. 'We made the grade playing that duet, didn't we?'

'Andre thought so. He couldn't stop talking about it afterwards, I noticed,' said Ann. 'It'll be good for you to have a break today, especially after the last few weeks.'

'Yes, but I can't relax wondering what bombshells await us next week,' Martha replied.

Ann pulled on her jacket and walked towards the front door. 'Come on—let's get out of the house. I'd like to take Scout for a run around the park at the end of the street. Coming?'

♫ ♫ ♫

Taking the Plunge

At Wednesday's practice, most people were present except for a cornet player and a man on tuba. Andre hushed the band and announced that a technician had been to the band room with Bob the previous day to repair the copier, which they could now use.

He then caught Martha's attention and went over some of the music pieces that needed photocopying.

'If you could quickly do that for me while I start the band off with a hymn, I'd be grateful, thanks, Martha.'

As she scurried off into the music library, Andre picked up his music folder and placed it on his stand.

'Right, band. For the Sacred Test Piece, I've swapped, *Abide With Me* for, *I'll Walk With God* instead. So, take it out of your black folder and place it into your contest folder.'

He picked up his baton from his stand and before he stepped up on the podium, he hesitated.

'Wait, a moment ... I need to say that a few of us have reason to believe that there is a prankster in our midst. If any of you know who could have smeared the toilet seat with ammonia to cause Will such suffering, I'd like to know about it.' The band went deathly still.

'Also—somebody must have deliberately thrown a spanner in the works and damaged the copier. It was only a small tool, but it has caused the band a huge expense.'

A woman put up her hand to speak. 'It could be the Junior Band who use the room twice a week. We all know there are some unruly teenagers with that lot,' she said.

'Not necessarily. They might be mischievous, but I doubt whether they would do this. Anyway—let's play music!' Andre retorted.

With that, he stepped up onto the podium and opened his folder glancing at the score.

Ann sat at the sideline, having cleaned up the cups in the kitchen and sat back to listen to one of her favourite hymns they were about to play.

Within seconds of his stepping onto the podium, a terrific crash reverberated as the platform collapsed sending Andre catapulting—music stand, scores and conductor's baton flying across the room almost landing in a horn player's lap.

'Ahh!' he bellowed across the room. 'My arm!' he moaned as he lay prostrate on the floor with his right arm at a strange angle.

People sprang out of their seats and rushed towards him, knocking over stands sending music sheets flying. Sandy, a competent first-aider yelled, 'call an ambulance,' after assessing his injuries.'

'No, please don't,' he muttered, his face screwing up in agony. 'You said it's just a broken arm. Someone can run me to the hospital—I don't need bells and whistles. Bob's here somewhere—see if he'll take me,' he groaned.

While someone searched for Bob, two of the men checked the podium and discovered someone had unscrewed the legs from underneath.'

Once they got Andre onto his feet, Bob arrived to take him to the hospital. If he hadn't been there, Ann was ready to offer to drive him.

'Ask Chad if he can conduct for me today. I'll be back on Friday, I guess,' he said to one of the horn players who sat in the front row and staggered out to Bob's car leaning on him with his good arm. His nose was bleeding, and someone had given him a gauze pack which he held against it once he had slumped into the vehicle.

While some people helped drag the podium out of the way and picked up Andre's music scattered across the room, Ann went over to inspect the offending platform. She could see that someone had interfered it with and took photos with her phone as she did when the cymbals had been glued together at the dress rehearsal.

'Just to keep a record for Martha,' she said to Terrence, the nosy horn player who stood over her watching what she was doing.

'Hmm—looks like someone unscrewed the legs and left the base resting on them. Only a psycho would do that!' he ranted.

'Come on, everyone—back to your seats,' Chad cried. 'Bob will sort this out, but let's finish our rehearsal, please.'

Martha sat in her seat with her cornet, giving Ann a sideways look. She responded by shaking her head to let her know that this situation had got out of control.

Ann felt sorry for Martha since the spate of malicious attacks had crushed her bubbly, positive disposition. Her friend had become a nervous wreck, trying hard to be optimistic—but Ann could see the cracks beginning to show. Colour had drained from her face, and tramlines had etched their way across her forehead.

♫ ♫ ♫

Martha woke to an early morning phone call from Andre.

'What's the verdict?' she asked.

'Well you've heard of a one-armed paper-hanger,' he said, chuckling.

'How are your injuries?'

'Not so bad, apart from a broken nose and busted arm. The only thing is, it's my principal conducting arm.'

'Oh, that's terrible. Does that mean you won't be able to make it to the contest?'

'Not at all. Wild horses won't stop me winning that cup. But I think we must consider getting a few cameras installed in the band room so we can catch this prankster red-handed.'

'Yes—I think that would be an excellent idea, except that they are horribly expensive. I had my son install them at my house, but just keep that to yourself please.'

'Is he a technical person?'

'He's an electronic technician. I could ask him if he would be interested in coming out to do the job, but he said he's pretty snowed under at present and lives miles away in Botany.'

'Oh, dear—yes, that is a fair distance from here. I will have to approach the committee and see if the coffer has sufficient funds. With all the materials we've had to buy after the fire damage, there may not be much money left, but I'll do my best to convince them. Our old hall had outside security lights which made a difference because the building could be seen from the road. Perhaps we could install lighting first and later cameras if we can afford it.'

Martha came off the phone relieved that her battered conductor could still make the contest. She hurried off to look for Ann to tell her the news.

'Oh, there you are,' Martha said, spotting Ann behind the picket fence that divided the backyard lawn and the flower garden.

'Hi there—I woke early, and it's such a lovely day I thought I'd do a bit of weeding and guess what? I caught your sweet Petticoat with her front legs on the picket fence trying to reach your sunflowers.'

'Silly goat—she's been trying to reach them for ages. When they finish flowering, I'll let her have them. By the way, Andre just called. He is recovering well from his injuries and says he'll approach the committee about installing cameras in the band room.'

'It might have a reverse effect, Martha. If it's a member of Riverlea Brassholes who is causing the trouble, once they know there are cameras, they may become extra cunning and perform their malice out of the band room. That will be more difficult to track, so it would be better if we could catch them in the act on the premises when they slip up.'

'I'll tell that to Andre,' Martha replied. 'To be honest, I don't think the band can afford it right now.'

Martha walked beside Ann as they strolled through the orchid behind Petticoat. 'Off you go!' she said to the goat, clapping her hands at the animal.

Ann took time out to catch up with her list of persons of interest and had narrowed it down significantly. But somehow, they needed to find out what was happening on the days that the Junior Band held their practices twice a week. Ann wasn't convinced that it could be a youth. Her suspicions veered more to a bitter member of the Brassholes who carried a vendetta.

She sat in the sun on the veranda out the back, perusing her dossier and adding notes she'd made from her black book. Martha had gone shopping in the city and would return late afternoon, which gave Ann a day without distractions. She made a call to DS Isaac Yule to touch base. Just as she had expected, he'd made no progress with his own investigations around the village and yonder, even after enquiring at butchers' shops in the area as to the origin of the piece of rump steak thrown to Scout that day. Isaac also listed several Medical Centres and Veterinarian Clinics where he had asked whether they kept the drug, *Acepro* on their premises. But all his investigations were futile.

Ann felt a weight on her shoulders. She rubbed her neck and then kneaded her shoulder muscles. The tension of the last three weeks was getting to her.

She got up to make herself another coffee and then realised it would not help her stress levels. Instead, she boiled the kettle to make a cup of chamomile tea with honey.

This case had dragged on too long. From the first sign of foul play with Martha getting locked in the library until now, the plot had thickened. It was more complicated than Ann had expected—and malicious.

Chapter Thirteen

'Sorry, Ann—my memory is getting worse these days. I forgot to tell you Andre phoned while I was out shopping yesterday. He was most insistent on getting the police out to the band room to investigate the spate of misdemeanours we've had. I didn't know how to tell him not to do that without saying an investigation was already underway, which I didn't.'

'That's wise, Martha. I know it's difficult to keep putting him off, but once the perpetrator knows he is under surveillance, he will stop his activity and may attack people in their homes instead.'

'I know how that feels. Why can't we tell Andre you're a retired Detective Inspector and now a private investigator? We can get his assurance that he won't breach our confidence, and then he will ward off the police.'

'I've been thinking of that myself. Andre appears to be a straight shooter and won't let us down. How about I ask him this afternoon if he could meet us here tomorrow to discuss it? It would probably be good to have someone else on board who is a witness to the vandalism, someone we can trust. He may even have some useful suggestions.'

♫ ♫ ♫

To Ann and Martha's surprise, there were no sinister offences at that afternoon's rehearsal. Andre struggled to conduct with his wrist in plaster, and although he still had the use of his fingers, he appeared awkward as he tried to shuffle through his music folder. That afternoon he didn't have the confidence to stand on the podium, although Bob checked he had fastened the legs securely before Andre arrived.

Chad, their lead cornet, played the solo, *You Raise Me Up* better than Ann had ever heard before. He will win the own selection piece, she thought.

After Martha helped Ann finish putting everything away in the kitchen, she walked over to pack up her music folders and cornet case ready to head home. She overheard Chad telling Andre and others that he would carry out repairs in the instrument room after assisting at the Junior Band practice on Saturday and will probably be there until late.

It thrilled Ann and Martha that Andre had agreed to drop by Martha's house on Saturday to discuss how they would handle the vicious assaults on band members, and Andre believed it wasn't prankish behaviour. Instead, they were the hateful actions of an adult holding a grudge; he had told Martha.

♫ ♫ ♫

It had been several years since middle-aged Andre had visited Martha at her home. He had been a close friend of Frank, her late husband and took his death badly as the older man had been like a father to him.

Martha fussed over him, bringing scones and tea out onto the veranda in the sun. Ann waited for Martha to broach the subject, but first, it seemed he wanted to reminisce over old times when Frank had been active in the band.

After morning tea and a guided tour around the garden and backyard, they returned to sit on the veranda soaking up the gentle, autumn sun.

'Let's get down to brass tacks,' said Martha. 'Ann and I have something we need to tell you—or at least, Ann does.'

Andre glanced at Martha sideways and then at Ann. 'Oh, I see. That sounds serious—fire away, Ann,' he nodded, with a warm smile.'

'You are looking at retired Detective Inspector, Ann Grieves. She's the real McCoy,' said Martha.

Andre sat gaping at Ann, waiting for her to show whether this was a joke.

'No, she's right. I retired from the police force several years ago, having served as a Detective Inspector in Southland after moving there from Auckland. I shifted back here when I left the service and now work part-time as a private investigator. Somehow I became hoodwinked into investigating this spate of criminal acts in your band room.'

'Is that right? Why didn't anyone tell me, Martha?'

Ann jumped in. 'Martha wanted to tell you, but I cautioned her not to. Any police involvement or overt investigative action at that stage would have pressured the culprit into using more devious tactics as he had done with Winnie and Scout. But it could have been worse. I want them to continue their acts of sabotage within the band room so that they'll hopefully slip up and we can catch them red-handed.'

'Goodness me. That has been going on under the radar. So, what is your plan if you don't want police involvement?'

'I'm not saying don't involve the police. I just suggest you delay that until we corner the villain, or we'll frighten them away. The same goes for the surveillance cameras. Once they see them, they may stay and start targeting band members in their homes.'

'Aw, I don't think they'd go that far, would they? It sounds like a bold trickster to me.'

Martha nodded at Ann. 'Tell him about Scout.'

Ann went into great depth about the attack on Scout and the cameras installed around Martha's property.

After they discussed the chain of events from when Martha was first locked in the library until Andre fell from the podium, he quietly digested the barrage of information.

Ann broke his silence. 'Andre—it's imperative at this point to say if you are aware of any bandsmen or bandswomen who might have a vendetta against the band. Could someone hold a grudge, as the attacks haven't just been on one person—they are directed at the whole band?'

'No, I can't think of anyone who would fall into that category—not at all,' said Andre, rubbing his finger over his chin.

'I think we need to get cameras installed throughout the entire building that will cover both our rehearsals and the Junior Band practices.'

'I understand. Just give me until after the contest,' said Ann. 'I think I can crack this one.'

'Fair enough. The committee isn't too keen on spending the money on cameras anyway, although they would consider getting security lights installed. I'll leave it up to you, and I'll keep quiet about it if you keep me informed. Sorry, I must get off now.'

Andre picked up his car keys from the table and headed towards the steps.

'Wait there a minute!' Martha darted into the kitchen and returned with a jar of preserves.

'Here—Golden Queen peaches from my orchard.'

'Thanks, that's kind of you—see you on Monday. Keep up your two-hours practice a day,' he said, with a wink and hurried off out to his car.

Chapter Fourteen

Only one week to go the contest and already Martha was worn out. Probably the rest of the band were too, she guessed, when she imagined the impact the unpleasant events must have had on the rest of the players.

'I'm so glad it's Sunday,' she said to Ann as they drove off to the quaint Anglican church in the village. 'I find it so calming when we sing the hymns, and the worship so uplifting.'

As they walked down the aisle to take a seat near the front, Ann caught sight of Isaac sitting near the back.

'I didn't know Isaac went to your church,' Ann whispered to Martha,' as they sat down.

'I think I recall him coming now and then, but I didn't know who he was until he came to my home that day. I still wasn't sure but said nothing,' said Martha, softly.

Ann tugged her sleeve. 'I think we'd better be quiet—it appears they're about to start.'

When the service ended, the women fetched themselves a cup of coffee served in the foyer. Isaac, who stood talking to a parishioner, glanced over at Martha and waved. He smiled at the person he was speaking to and walked over towards Ann and Martha, as they put their cups on the tea trolley.

'I was hoping to catch up with you soon. I hear from one of your bandsmen there has been foul play going on with your band,' he said to Martha. 'I was wondering why no one reported it.'

Martha darted a glance at Ann and raised her eyebrows.

'Oh, that. Yes, we have had a bit of skulduggery going on, but we're managing it internally. It may be some of the pranksters from the Junior Band,' Martha stammered, feeling guilty about twisting the truth, especially while at church.

Ann interjected. 'It's all under control, but if we need any backup, we'll be in touch.'

'Ah, yes–Calamity Ann, I heard you have been in the game yourself—a high-ranking officer of note. You said nothing.'

Ann squirmed. 'It's … um—I am retired and doing a bit of private investigating. I didn't even think to mention it.'

Martha jumped in to rescue her. 'And we don't want police involvement at this stage. There are a few disruptive youths in that band, and we'll deal with them.'

Isaac gave a half-smile. 'And you think the meat in your backyard was an isolated incident?'

He didn't wait for the women to answer and took his cup out to the kitchen. They waved to him as they walked out to the car park.

'Sounds as though Isaac thinks the culprit in the band room is the same person who threw that meat to Scout,' said Martha.

'Oh, yes, for sure. He will have gathered that I'm doing the investigation and keeping him at arm's length. Never mind—we don't need him at this point.'

'I knew it wouldn't take long in a tiny village like this for word to get around about the trouble we've had with the band,' said Martha.

'And it was inevitable Isaac would find out I'm an ex-police officer,' Ann replied.

'To be honest, Ann. It's getting risky since Andre's fall. He could have come off a lot worse. I'm afraid of what that unbalanced psycho could do next.'

They stepped into Ann's vehicle and continued the conversation.

'Look—if it makes you feel happier, get the cameras installed in the band room next week. At least it will catch someone tampering with our equipment.'

Martha glanced at Ann's solemn face. 'That's good, isn't it?'

'The only thing is—like I said, instead of carrying out their deeds at band, they'll become more deceptive and ruthless, stalking people at home.'

'I get it. Perhaps we'd best hold off on the cameras for now.'

Chapter Fifteen

Death By Tuba

Ann and Martha were early to band practice on Monday, just as Andre pulled into the car park. As they climbed out of Martha's car, Winnie arrived with the milk.

'You're early today, Winnie—all set for the contest on Saturday?' asked Martha with a cheery smile.'

'As ready as I'll ever be. With all the animals on the farm to look after and hubby recently getting over the flu, I've hardly had time for two hours practice a day. To be honest, it's getting a bit nerve-wracking now.'

'Don't talk to me about nerve-wracking,' said Martha, winking at Ann.

'Look—that's Chad's car parked over there, isn't it?' she said to Winnie. He must have arrived early, but how did he get in without a key?' mumbled Martha, with Andre in tow as she traipsed up the steps into the band room. She dumped her cornet case and music satchel on a chair.

'He probably borrowed Matt's key,' said Andre. As he wandered around the band room drawing curtains and turning on lights, he noticed a glow emanating from the instrument room. Walking closer to check it out, he stopped aghast by the door. 'What the?' he bellowed. 'Help! Someone, call an ambulance … no … call the police!'

Those were the only words he could utter. White as a sheet, he collapsed on a chair holding his throat and pointing at the room where the door was half-ajar.

'What is it?' Martha asked, with the others in tow, rushing towards him.

They hadn't worked out that Andre wasn't the person in trouble, although he was still holding his throat.

'Instrument room … quick… look!' he gasped.

Ben, the secretary, had arrived and raced to help with the others following behind. There, face-down on the floor lay Chad, the lead cornet player—prostate and lifeless with a tuba lying across his shoulders smeared with blood.

Ben checked his vital signs, feeling for a pulse in his neck. He glanced up as Ann arrived next to him and shook his head at her.

'I'm a trained first-aider, let me look,' she said.

Ben gladly moved aside as Ann also felt for a pulse and examined the back of Chad's head revealing thick, congealed blood amongst the matted black hair on the back of his scalp. She leaned his head to one side, exposing his face, which was the colour of a blue-bottle jellyfish and shuddered, pulling her hand away from his ice-cold cheek.

Martha hovered by the doorway.

Ann glanced at the onlookers. 'It appears he's been dead for a while,' Ann said. 'Has anyone called the police?'

'They're on their way,' said Winnie, who poked her head around the door and slapped her hand over her mouth in horror. 'Oh, no, poor Chad. How did this happen?'

'Sorry, Winnie. Could you call again and tell them the man is dead? They'll need to bring a police doctor with them to confirm it.'

By this time Andre had calmed himself and ambled gingerly over to where they stood, the colour still drained from his face.

'He was working until late Saturday evening repairing instruments, poor beggar,' he stammered. He's been in here for two days.'

'Mmm, smells like it,' whispered Winnie in Martha's ear.

'Looks like that tuba fell off the shelf from up there and smacked him over the head,' said Ben, pushing it aside.

Ann lurched forward. 'Wait, all of you—don't touch anything! This is a case for the police—you can't make any assumptions it was the tuba. It could be something worse.'

Ben grimaced and stood up out of the way.

'You're right,' he said. 'That deep gash in his head looks suspect. I can't image a tuba would make a hole like that.'

Andre sat slumped in a seat outside the room with his head hanging low while Martha sidled up to him.

'I guess this puts an end to our rehearsal today. It couldn't get much worse than this, could it?' he muttered with a quaver in his voice. 'After all the work we've put into the contest.'

Martha, instead of comforting him felt a twinge of anger rise inside her, as Andre only worried about the contest.

'He may not have had a wife and family, but there'll be a few bandsmen who'll take this hard,' she blurted uncontrollably, aware she'd snapped at him.'

Andre just sat there looking at his feet and shaking his head, muttering away to himself.

Most of the band members rallied around announcing the bad news to their comrades who had traipsed through the front door arriving amidst the uproar. Ann cautioned everyone that the band room was now a crime scene, and they would have to clear the area when the police arrive.

Chapter Sixteen

When a siren sounded as a police vehicle veered into the car park, a spirit of heaviness fell with a thud inside Ann's soul. Had she spoken out of turn when she'd encouraged Martha to persuade the committee to delay installing video cameras in the band room? Perhaps her plan for holding back on catching the criminal red-handed had something to do with pride. She continued to remonstrate with herself.

The police arrived promptly, rushing through the door as if there was a fire to put out. They raced to the suspected crime scene and requested the straggling by-standers to move away and sit down.

A six-foot-tall, strapping Irishman took up half the room with his arms spread-eagled lying flat on his face. The police officer in charge requested that everyone take their seats, apart from Andre and the few people who'd found Chad. Other officers fired a multitude of questions at the conductor who was still shaken, stuttering and stammering his way through the ordeal. Another police officer was on the phone to a detective.

'Please stay here,' said the senior police officer to Ann, Martha and Winnie, as they talked amongst themselves about the cause of Chad's injuries. 'We need to ask you all a few questions. The detective will be here soon.'

Martha glanced at her comrades and could see they were still in shock as she was. 'Mind if I make us all a cup of tea? We usually have one at this time before we start a practice,' she implored the police officer.

'Sorry, I don't want you to touch anything, as we are treating this as a crime scene. Once we get all your contact details, you must vacate the building.'

Martha glanced at Ann, who hovered nearby. 'You don't look too good, Ann,' Martha said, scanning her strained face.

'I suppose I didn't expect the offender to go this far—It will be a forensics case now.'

Before long, the detective turned up, rushing through the door straight to the police officers. Ann's face flushed the colour of a lobster as she saw DS Isaac Yule fronting up to the scene looking for clues.

The women followed and stood at the door as he edged his way into the instrument room. He looked down at Chad then scanned the room—the various instruments and leather cases on the shelves. Pulling on a pair of gloves he extracted from his pocket, he bent down to inspect the injury to Chad's scalp.

Andre mulled around nearby, trying to take it all in.

'What will happen with my tuba now?' asked Monty, standing with his hands on his hips by the door. That's my instrument Chad was repairing, and he said that it would be ready for today's practice. It's covered in blood. Will they take it away somewhere?' he grumbled.

Andre frowned at him. 'I don't think there'll be any practice going on today, do you?' he growled.

Monty glared back at him. 'Well, that does me for the contest then!'

'There are plenty of other tubas you can use. We must tell the detective you need to take one. Come on, Monty—don't go on. You can see we have other instruments on the shelf in mint condition which you can use. Let's just get through today and not worry about the contest.'

Isaac overheard and responded to the man's anxiety.

'We won't be taking your tuba away, but forensics will be here before long and take some blood and hair samples from it for testing. Once they've cleaned it, they will release the instrument. It looks like there's not only a dent in your poor buddy's head, but there's also one in your tuba—now can you ALL please sit down!'

That didn't amuse Monty.

Isaac greeted Ann, saying she could assist him with this case if she wished. She guessed he trusted her judgement and could do with back-up seeing his own Detective Inspector was out of action since a recent assault, he'd told her.

'I'll duck outside and cordon off the car park. This building will be out of bounds while it is a crime scene, and we are locking the gate. A scene guard will keep watch while forensics carry out their job.'

'That'll be interesting,' said Martha, joining the conversation.

'Everyone listen up!' said Andre, who perked up suddenly. 'We must forego the practice today and instead we'll be back here Wednesday and Friday. It's a terrible time rehearsing under these sad circumstances, but just remind yourselves that Chad would want you to go for that cup without him.'

There was an unnerving silence when Andre spoke, and for once the band was lost for words. Martha knew how much the Sylvester Cup meant to everyone but was this going over the top. Then again— the group had worked so hard for months giving up precious family time to commit. She shrugged her doubts away.

Isaac stopped in the doorway, overhearing Andre's announcement and turned to face the sombre group. 'Sorry, folk, I don't want to spoil your rehearsals, but this building will be out of bounds until we have completed our forensic testing, so perhaps delay your practice until Friday. We don't want people traipsing contamination in or taking evidence out of the crime scene.'

Martha turned to Andre. 'Goodness—where are we going to conduct our rehearsals with only four days to go till the contest?'

'I don't know … except … maybe there is a place—Riverlea Community Hall. Local groups can use it, and they only charge a minimal fee. Maybe they'll let us in there for two sessions before Saturday. I'll phone the booking clerk tonight.'

Isaac and a police officer cordoned off the fence around the carpark and the main door of the building with yellow banners which read, *Crime Scene Do Not Cross*. They informed Andre that the forensics team were on their way.

'The crime scene investigators and coroner will be all over this place soon. Your members will have to evacuate the building once our officers have all your contact details.'

'So, is that it?' asked Martha. 'Aren't you going to interview each person separately?'

'Once we get the lab tests back, We must do our homework with the help of you and your conductor first, to see if anyone is a person of interest. I must get some details from you about the vandalism incidents you mentioned have taken place recently.'

'What about Ann? She has been investigating these incidents.'

Isaac smiled. 'I could do with Ann's help, as I've already told her. But you, Martha, have been in the band the longest and can supply me with vital information.'

Ann nodded in agreement, smiling at Martha.

'Oh, I forgot to tell you. Someone had smashed the front passenger window of Chad's vehicle. That's if it belongs to him as you say it does. It may have been a robbery, Martha, so you and Andre check if anything is missing. Did you notice anything else had been disturbed, and do you keep money in the building?'

'No, we don't keep money on the property, and Chad was the instrument custodian. He would have been the person to ask about the inventory and whether they were all there,' said Martha, beginning to snivel.

'The crime scene investigators or forensics team could be out of here before Wednesday afternoon, but I won't know until they have completed their initial assessment. When they have finished, I'll examine the rest of the area for clues. But I think you should not plan to use the building until Friday, just to be safe,' said Isaac. 'When they give you permission to re-enter the band room, I want you to look at your instrument inventory and tell me if they have stolen any.'

'Well, I suppose it's an obvious motive for murder. The tubas and euphoniums together could pay for a deposit on a house,' Andre muttered.

'Yes, I guess they would be worth killing for, in some criminal's eyes,' said Isaac. 'But we can't make assumptions, and that's why we have crime scene investigators who conduct forensic science. We don't know yet.'

Before long, the officers finished gathering contact details of all band members and then asked everyone to vacate the premises.

After they'd all left, a constable was about to lock the gate when a van carrying a battalion of forensic investigators arrived. They climbed out of the police vehicle dressed in white boiler suits carrying crime scene boxes, cameras and various gadgets, while Martha looked on shaking her head in disbelief. Ann joined her at the doorstep.

Martha cringed. 'I've never seen anything like it. They look like astronauts, and this feels like a science fiction movie in our local band room!'

Ann placed her hand on Martha's shoulder. 'This is normal with forensic investigations. They are wearing protective clothing so as not to corrupt the scene and for their own protection. We must leave now, Isaac said. I can work with him solving this case once he finishes with the scene investigators, as I'm not officially an investigating officer. Let's get out of here.'

They waved to Isaac as he directed Andre to the door who followed them out to the car park.

'I'll be in touch about the results of the forensic tests,' Isaac called from the doorstep and then went back inside.

As they stepped into Martha's car, Andre hurried over and tapped her on the shoulder.

'I don't know where this is all going to end—I never thought the culmination of the suspicious acts would come to this.'

'Yes, it's hard to believe. We really will have to get those cameras installed—I'll talk to my son about it. Seeing we are a community band, he may just charge us for materials and petrol as he lives a distance away in Botany.'

'Thanks, Martha. The committee will have no choice but to agree now.'

'It could save another life, and I would hate to think who could be next,' said Martha, glumly.

Ann felt a load of guilt weigh heavily on her, pressing against her chest wall. She heaved a sigh as she let her breath go.

'Come on, Ann. You look done in—let's go home. It has been a tiresome day.'

For the first time in Ann's lengthy career as a detective, and more recently as a private investigator, a foreboding uneasiness in her spirit rocked her self-confidence. Had she been remiss in the advice she'd given Martha in keeping the malicious attacks under wraps? Maybe she's beginning to lose her touch or worse—getting past it. She felt sick in the stomach at the prospect of losing her grip.

Chapter Seventeen

Sorry, Martha, but I'm off to bed. I'm completely done in after today—I'm not a spring chicken anymore. Perhaps I should rest like you,' Ann chuckled, winking as she gathered up her spectacles and day book.'

'I'm just preparing a cup of hot milk and honey—it helps me sleep. Would you like me to bring you one?'

'That sounds wonderful,' said Ann. 'I'd like to try it for a change—I hear it settles the nerves.'

Ann couldn't wait to get off her feet. She got into her pyjamas and went into the ensuite bathroom, peering into the mirror as she took out her toothbrush. For the first time in months, black moons underlined her eyes and crow's feet had formed in the corners— wrinkles she hadn't seen before.

Ready for bed, she picked up her case dossier and climbed under the duvet.

There was a gentle tap on the door.

'Okay if I come in?'

'Sure—I'm in bed.'

Martha carried a small tray with a mug of hot milk. 'Try it and see if it's sweet enough?'

She took a sip. 'Lovely—thanks. It's exactly right.'

Martha turned to leave the room.

'Don't go if you have a minute—there's something I need to talk to you about that has been eating away at me since Chad's death. Come and sit down,' Ann said, patting the foot of the bed.

'Sure, no problem.' Martha re-tied her pink, candlewick dressing gown, smoothed out the duvet and sat down.

Ann took a few sips of the milk and cleared her throat. 'I think I've been remiss in deterring you from asking the committee to install video cameras in the band room. Perhaps you should have done that after the first few incidents. I just waited, thinking if it were one of your band members who held a grudge, it would have been obvious, and I would have been able to drive them into a corner and catch them red-handed. That's how we used to do it in the force, in my day. I'm not used to solving crimes with all these CCTV cameras.'

'But surely that makes it a lot easier, and it provides you with concrete evidence too.'

'I know it might sound strange to you, Martha, but to me, it feels like cheating—that there's no point being a detective if all we do is put cameras everywhere to catch them in the act.'

'I suppose so, but I wouldn't know what it would be like in your shoes,' said Martha.

'Look—I can now see their worth in other instances, but in this case—I'm not sure. Oh, I'd better swig this milk down before it gets cold,' Ann said, picking up the mug clasping it to test the temperature.

'Why do you think a camera may not work in our situation?' Martha asked yawning.

'I'd say you would probably only have one camera sufficient to cover all the entrances to the rooms in that building. It's not as if it would be a hidden camera. If the culprit were a member of your band, they would probably be cunning enough to smear the camera lens with peanut butter or jam, or disable it with a laser pointer, especially if they are bold enough to murder. Burglars often disable security cameras.'

'I see ... you mean they would have been able to get away with their criminal acts whether there was a camera in the building or not.'

'The sabotage of the copier and the chemical attack was done out of sight. If there had been a camera in the band room, it would have spotted someone tampering with the equipment. As I said, if anyone knew there was CCTV in the building, they might have changed their mind and attacked players in their own homes instead.'

'So, you're saying that even if we had installed a camera right from the beginning, it might not have deterred the offender?'

Ann started rubbing her eyes and glanced at her watch.

'Even with cameras, burglars and other criminals carry out crimes hiding their faces. Professionals wear a balaclava or hoodie which will conceal their identity.'

'But if they left the building, they'd be detected on camera getting into their car,' said Martha, her voice beginning to fade.

'If they are sharp and desperate enough to disable an inside camera, they would make sure they have got to the outside one and taken care of that first.'

Martha stood with her hands behind, arching her back. 'I'm tuckered out now. All this is giving me a headache. I don't know how you did this for so many years.'

'You mean detective work? It was my passion— I was born for it,' Ann said, with a warm smile. 'Let's get some sleep. We've got a way to go before we get on top of this lot. The results of the tests will be interesting.'

Chapter Eighteen

Following the lengthy discussion with Martha the previous night about security cameras, Ann woke with a heavy head despite having slept right through.

Her mind was racing and giving her disturbing flashbacks of Chad lying dead in the instrument room. A case like this rarely unsettled her to that degree. But she had got to know him a little since spending time with the band. She'd become familiar with most of the musicians, and perhaps that's why she'd downplayed the incidents until Chad's death.

As Ann drew the curtains, bright sun rays streamed into her room, causing her to squeeze her eyes shut. Reluctant to get out of bed, she hoped to lie in a little longer.

Today she would go through the history of each band member which she had compiled during the past three weeks, as there had to be something she had missed. It had become more than evident that this was an inside job. Still, the motive—that would be a significant challenge, as Ann had discreetly assessed every player through talking to them separately. They all appeared to be amicable and transparent, but she knew well from decades of dealing with sociopaths, that wolves come in attractive, counterfeit sheep's clothing.

She dressed and went along to the dining room, where she heard Martha setting the table.

'You're up already? I expected you to sleep in after yesterday's fiasco,' she said. 'Let me make breakfast. What about French toast?'

'Oh, you need not do that. Why don't you go and relax? You need brain food, as it works overtime, I'm sure,' said Martha sweetly.

'No, please, Martha. It will help me focus and centre myself for the day. Do you like French Toast?'

'I do. I've only eaten it at cafés when Frank used to take me out for breakfast, but I've never cooked it myself.'

'Well, let me spoil you. I bought some blueberries from the berry farm near the village, and we can have it with honey and Greek yoghurt. I planned to do it one day this week.'

'Alright, if you insist.'

'If you don't mind, I need to talk to you and discuss my plan to visit each band member so I can compile a proper criminal personality profile on each one—even those I believe are not persons of interest. It has been a little difficult to do it in the band room on tea break each practice when there is little time, and it needs to be private. You must make sure you have told me every single personal detail you know about each player—even if you think it's unimportant.'

'That sounds like a workload—but can you do that if you aren't an official part of the investigating team?'

'Absolutely—in fact, Isaac has asked if I would assist in interviewing each band member as possible witnesses and collect as much evidence as I can. His department is overloaded after the recent terrorist attack in West Auckland. It is perfectly legal for private investigators to help the police, so don't worry, I won't be getting into any kind of trouble.'

'That's great news. I'll make the coffee while you do your French Toast. I'm looking forward to tasting it, and then after we've eaten, get your dossier, and we'll go over everything sitting out under the umbrella on the veranda. It's such glorious weather.'

♫ ♫ ♫

'Bring your drink out here, Ann. It's lovely in the early autumn sun—so mild,' said Martha, planting herself down at the table under the umbrella. She moved into a seat in the sun and rolled her sleeves up. Minutes later, Ann returned with her dossier and a mug of coffee. She sat down perusing the notes she'd written.

'By process of availability and feasibility, I have narrowed the list of probable suspects down to only four out of twenty band members. But I want to make sure I'm on the right track and will begin visiting each person at their home, as I'll have to interview the whole band in case someone has slipped through the cracks.'

'Let's go through each member's background history now, one by one. I'll tell you what I know about each individual, and if you have gaps in the information you've already recorded, you can add it.'

'That's the idea—and I can compare the notes I have collected to see if we might find a red herring amongst them and go from there.'

'It sounds like we'll be in for the long haul, so I think I'll go inside and get dressed before I feed the hens, and then I'm all yours.'

'Thanks, Martha. After we've finished, I'll visit Tom—the one you said had donated the building to the band. I know his house is secluded and he probably can't see much from where he lives, but there's a chance he may have observed unusual activity in the area, even an isolated vehicle parked by the band room.'

'Marvellous idea—I'll be back in a jiffy.'

Chapter Nineteen

Ann carried a small, document satchel through into the dining room where Martha stood wiping down the table. 'Why don't you come along with me? I've only met Tom once in passing when I wandered through the orchard one day. He most likely won't remember me and will feel more comfortable answering my questions if you are there, seeing he knows you well.'

'Are you sure? I thought I'd be in the way. I'll get my jacket—I won't be long.' Martha turned to walk away and then stopped short. 'Tell you what ... I know of a shortcut through a narrow walkway between my two neighbouring properties. It leads out onto the street the band room is located, on Tom's side of the orchard. We could walk as it's only about fifteen minutes from here.'

'Sounds like a good plan to me. I'll change into my walking shoes.'

'Why don't you bring Scout too? He'd love to get out for a bit, wouldn't he?'

'As long as Tom won't mind—although he'll be on a lead so should be no trouble.'

When Ann returned wearing suitable shoes, Martha hurried back to get her jacket, and by the time she locked the house and reached the gate, Ann was waiting for her on the street with Scout on the lead.

'Oh, darn,' Martha said, as she opened the gate. Wait there—I've got to go back inside for my sunhat. That's the trouble with having fair skin.'

While Martha scurried back to unlock the door and fetch her hat, Ann inspected the new flowers she'd planted at the front of the section, bending down looking for bugs. Unbeknown to her, Hyacinth escaped through the gate and disappeared around the corner to feast on Martha's shrubs.

Martha arrived with her sunhat covered in artificial daffodils. 'Sorry to hold you up.' She closed the gate behind her, before showing Ann her straw sunhat. 'I collect the daffodils every year when I donate to the Cancer Foundation—quite a collection.'

Ann glanced at the hat and chuckled. 'I phoned Tom earlier to let him know we'll be dropping by. He's expecting us.'

They took the path that Martha had suggested—along a narrow walkway with hedges either side and now and then a house appeared. Just as they reached the end of the long track, Martha bent down to retie her shoelace and froze.

'Hyacinth! What the dickens are you doing here?' she blurted. 'How did you get out? Come here!' She lurched forwards in horror grabbing the pig by the scruff of her neck as she began to demolish what looked like a specimen camellia shrub covered in deep red flowers—one that had been carefully manicured and likely to be the apple of somebody's eye.

'What am I going to do? I can't be bothered walking back, and how am I going to control her?' snapped Martha, standing hands-on-hips, shaking her head at her pet.

Ann bent over to Scout. 'Here boy, let's help poor Martha out,' she said, as she unfastened Scout's collar from around his neck.

She turned to Martha handing her the collar and lead.

'Put this on her and take her with us. Scout is well-controlled off a lead, being an ex-police dog. He'll trot along next to me. You'll just have to fasten her to a small tree or something when we get to Tom's house.'

'Thanks, so much for that. She must have slipped out when I went inside for my sunhat. I thought I'd secured the latch on the gate but couldn't have.'

Ann struggled to stop laughing out loud at the unusual sight of Martha walking along the track leading a spotty, pink pig while the dog was off the lead. Especially when they arrived on the main street where they still had a two hundred metre walk along the side of the road on a narrow footpath. Ann cringed imagining what passers-by and car passengers would think.

Martha pulled on the pig's lead. 'You've made me look like the village idiot now, haven't you, Hyacinth? Some people would threaten you with pork roast for doing this.'

Both women laughed heartily.

'Poor Hyacinth. I think you've hurt her feelings,' said Ann, finding it difficult to remove the broad grin from her face until they arrived at Tom's house.

'Here we are,' said Martha, as she walked right up to a rusty harrow and secured Hyacinth, pulling on the lead just to make sure she couldn't get away again.

'He doesn't have any mean dogs, does he? Otherwise, Hyacinth could be looking at the slow cooker, for sure,' said Ann, with a sympathetic chuckle.

'Nope—just an old Labrador dog who doesn't leave his side and is placid as a lamb. But I'd bet if anyone tried to hurt Tom, that dog would rip them apart,' said Martha. 'Perhaps it would be best to ask him where you could put Scout while you're visiting.'

Tom was delighted to see them, and with a glance, Martha noticed he'd spruced himself up. It was probably the first visit from any women in a long while. After they explained what had happened with

Hyacinth, Tom brought his dog, Blossom, outside to meet Scout. The two dogs sniffed their approval playfully.

'Now go on your mat, Blossom! Inside you go.'

Tom directed the women inside into his lounge while his dog plonked itself down on the mat next to the empty fireplace. Scout sidled over to her while she sniffed him once more and then lay still, gazing at him.

'If I'm sitting in my armchair, she won't move from the mat as though she's watching over me. She follows me wherever I go.'

Martha bent over and patted Blossom's head. 'She's a great companion, I see.'

Take a seat over there, both of you. Won't be long before we need a fire. Days are drawing in slowly now. I've got the kettle on if you'd like a brew, but I've only got tea, sorry. Haven't done my weekly shop yet and ran out of coffee.'

'Thanks, Tom. Don't go to any trouble, please,' said Martha, feeling sorry for the old man who'd lived a reclusive life his wife had died.

'Here, Tom,' said Martha. She put her hand inside a calico shopping bag she carried and pulled out a small bundle. 'I made some blueberry muffins. I've taken them from the freezer, so just heat them in the microwave, and they'll be as fresh as if I baked them today.'

'Ah, thank you,' he said, opening the tea-towel Ann had wrapped them in. 'A microwave has been a godsend since Beryl I lost Beryl. I haven't had a blueberry muffin since she baked them,' he said, placing them on the bench. He removed a packet of biscuits from his pantry and arranged them on a plate.

'Sorry, not as elaborate as yours, but they're tasty.'

'Tim Tams—they're my favourites,' said Ann, taking one and handing the plate to Martha who also indulged.

'Now—what brings you here?' asked Tom after he poured the tea. 'You didn't say much except you needed to see me, and by the tone in your voice that spelt trouble.'

'Oh, I'm sorry if I put you on edge, Tom,' said Ann. 'Martha and I need to tell you about a bit of trouble we've had at the band room, in fact, some awful news.'

The two women talked at length describing each malicious attack on the band members, as Tom sat aghast, listening speechless to every mystifying detail. He jumped in when there was a gap in their patter.

'I'm sorry to hear the dire news. Is there anything I can do to help?' Tom asked, patting Blossom's head while Scout demanded his attention too, licking his hand. Tom tickled him under his neck while Ann and Martha smiled at him warmly.

'Apart from any other night, we need to find out if anyone saw a vehicle in the band room car park last

Saturday evening when Chad was murdered. You know his vehicle, don't you?'

'Yep, that is the flashy, blue Ford Mondeo. You couldn't miss that, but unfortunately, I can't see much from here, as that orange grove of mine blocks it.'

Ann got up and peered out his lounge window while Martha turned and craned her neck to see.

'You're right—mostly secluded from here all along the fence line. I can barely see the roof of the building, but you have a small view of the entrance to the car park. Apart from that, you are pretty much tucked away here.'

'Yep, Beryl and I made it so. When the packhouse was in operation, we used dozens of contractors from all over New Zealand and from overseas. They were seasonal workers for three months of the year. Beryl and I valued our privacy, and with young children, we needed our security too. That's why we planted a row of evergreen citrus trees along the fence line.'

'Did you ever see any suspicious activity when you drove past the band room or hear anything out of the ordinary?'

'Not that I can remember. I only drive into the village and back and usually go the back way, not past the band room. I'm sorry, I don't seem to be much help, but I hope you track down this loose cannon, whoever they are.'

Ann and Martha were deflated. Ann called Scout as they thanked Tom for the tea and headed off outside with him in tow after he left his dog shut inside the house.

'Wait, a moment—there is something. I've just had a bit of a flashback.'

Ann's face lit up. 'What is it—you mean you've seen something?'

'It may not be anything, but you asked if I noticed any unusual activity in the band room.'

He leaned against the closed door.

'There is something I recall catching my attention—unusual activity, I suppose.'

'What do you mean, Tom?' asked Martha.

'Even though I can't see the whole of the band room's car park from here, I can vaguely see the top half of the building and the entrance to the parking area, especially at night when the lights are on.'

He directed the women to a wooden bench under a cherry tree to shield them from the sun, while Hyacinth, who was on the elasticized dog lead, tried to reach them from a short distance away.

'I know that the Junior Band use the building on Tuesday evenings and usually pack up around 9 pm, as I'm aware when they turn the lights off. Sometimes I've had to phone Matt, the conductor when someone has left a light on.'

Ann was getting agitated, as he was slow getting to the point.

'Well, last week something strange was going on after they switched off the lights and left the hall. I could hear several cars leave the car park as usual and then everything went quiet.'

'That was the night before Andre fell from the podium after the platform had been sabotaged!' cried Martha. 'What was unusual about that night, Tom?'

About an hour later, I heard a vehicle enter the parking area, and the lights were back on—or should I say I saw a glimmer of light through the trees in the distance. I thought I'd better check it out with Blossom, and we walked along the tree line bordering the fence on the boundary of my orchard until I found a gap in the branches. From my viewpoint, the light in the building was dim. I gathered that someone had forgotten something, and when they entered the hall, they couldn't find the light mains and used a strong pen torch instead.'

'How strange,' said Martha. 'The main switch is by the front door.'

'We walked back home, and it seemed whoever it was must have been in the building for almost an hour before I heard a vehicle start up and drive off.'

'You didn't think to give me a call to check it out?' asked Martha frowning.

'No, I didn't think it could be anyone else other than a band member trying to locate something they'd left behind. I even thought that the lights might have blown a fuse. I'm sorry, Martha. I feel as though I've let you down.'

'Oh, no—not at all. How were you to know that someone was in there sabotaging Andre's podium? The only thing that baffles me is how they managed to get a key.'

'Mmm, that's what we're going to find out. If the imposter managed to obtain a key and get it cut, that answers how they got into the building to carry out the rest of the destruction,' said Ann, finishing off writing her report and closing her notebook before placing it back into her document satchel.

'There's something else I can recall that may or may not be anything.'

'Spit it out, Tom. We need anything you can remember that made you think something didn't sit right,' said Ann,' fishing her book out of her bag again to take notes.

'At odd times, when I was sure the band practice was over, I caught sight of a white, Commodore long-wheelbase Ute from where I stood near the fence.'

'I don't know anyone at band with a vehicle like that. When was this?' asked Martha.

'I didn't take note of the days or times, but I've seen the same Ute pull into the car park when there was no one else there. I guessed it was one of your players working on the grounds or doing maintenance.'

Martha racked her brains, trying to remember what tradesmen would be there with a key.

'No one would have access except Bob and those of us who've had keys allocated. A band member always chaperones tradesmen.'

'Well, it remains an enigma, I guess. You ladies have some detective work to do,' said Tom.

'We'd better head back now, Martha,' said Ann. 'I've left my cell phone in my room, and Isaac said he would phone this afternoon with the forensic results.'

As Martha went to untie Hyacinth, she looked aghast, as the pig had dug a massive hole in the lawn. Her face turned crimson with embarrassment.

'I'm so sorry, Tom. I'll take her home and return later in my car to fix this. I have some topsoil at home to fill the hole. She was most likely getting bored.'

'Don't you worry yourself over this—it's trivial compared to the worries you have on your mind at present. Instead of that, how about giving an old fellow a visit occasionally—especially with those berry muffins,' he said winking at her. Her cheeks glowed this time, but not through embarrassment.

Martha knew that Tom was around her age as he had been a close friend of her late husband, Frank, although years of toiling in the sun and wind had made him appear a decade older.

'Mmm—one would think he might have designs on you,' said Ann, as they walked along the track back home. 'I haven't seen a smile on your face that big since I came to stay with you. Perhaps you should take him up on his offer, once all this has blown over.'

Martha's high colour and beaming smile stayed with her the entire walk home.

Chapter Twenty

Ann, it's the landline for you. Take it in my office if you want,' Martha called up the passageway.

'Darn—I must have had my phone on mute,' Ann called, checking her mobile as she walked into the office.

After a long conversation with Isaac, Ann traipsed into the dining room with her shoulders slumped, looking at the ground shaking her head.

'Oh dear, not the results you hoped for?' said Martha, clearing up the dinner dishes. 'I've boiled the kettle. Let's talk about it over a cuppa.'

She began pouring tea into bone china cups which she only brought out occasionally. 'Sit down and tell me the news.'

Martha handed the cup and saucer to Ann who hadn't drunk out of anything like that in decades, as she was a *worn-out mug* person.

'I can't believe what Isaac just told me. The tests have yielded negative results. The blood on the tuba was Chad's who had probably been smacked on the head with an iron bar or other metal object to make such a hole in his skull. It sounds as though someone had lost their temper.'

Martha paled. 'Jeepers! To think that there is a psychopathic killer in our band.' She shivered.

'It's horrible–I know, and it's my job to track them down. I won't give up until the villain is behind bars, Martha. Don't you worry.'

'I hope it happens soon as I'm becoming afraid.'

'Well, I'll just have to stay with you until it blows over. These people always trip themselves up, as it appears to be an amateur, not a serial killer. Their motive is to disable the band, but we need to find out why.'

'How are you going to do that—it could be any number of things?'

'I know—it can be a complicated journey of many twists and turns, and I'm ready for the ride. You just stay on board too and don't give up as you might miss something,' said Ann, trying to keep Martha focused.

'I need to see Matt, the Junior Band conductor at home, as I need to question him and can't do it around other band members,' said Ann.

'You don't suspect him, do you?'

'Not at all. Do you know whether he keeps a record of your players who attend the Junior Band to help them out? I hear that several of them do that, and I need their names.'

'That shouldn't be difficult. I'll go through the minutes of our recent committee meetings as there would be a record of who offered tuition and playing support. I remember who some of them are, but to be sure, I'll check the meeting reports. You can verify that with Matt.'

'Of course. I think it's time that Matt and I had a wee chat.'

'Yes, I think so too. Would you like me to come along?'

'Yes, I would, thanks, Martha. If I am to interview band members, I need to justify my reasons.'

'How will you do that without revealing you're a private investigator?'

'I'll have to be discreet. Andre has given me his word he won't disclose it to anyone until I give him the go-ahead. I'll need your help, and if we can visit each person together, you could tell them we are assisting Isaac with his investigation.'

'Sounds like it could work. I've never been involved in a police enquiry before. It's kind of exciting as well as scary.'

Ann smiled. 'Let me take the lead and ask the questions. I just want you to back me up. Imagine if you and I track down the killer—wouldn't that be one for the books?'

'What would you like me to do? Should I phone Matt next and make a time to see him? I'll just say I can't discuss it over the phone.'

'Yes, if you don't mind. We need to get onto it as soon as possible. Isaac said you could have your band room back again on Wednesday—the forensic team have clean it. He asked if you could get that instrument inventory to him as soon as possible and let him know what's missing.'

'Oh, dear—something else to do. That will take me a while—can you help?'

'Of course. Can you ask Matt to meet us at the band room? We can get there early in the morning before he arrives and kill two birds with one stone.'

'Oh, please don't say that K-word. You put my teeth on edge.'

'Sorry—I guess I've become a bit immune to it all.'

Chapter Twenty-one

Ann and Martha had got used to packing themselves sandwiches to take to band practice. There was always some reason for them to arrive early, and Martha couldn't believe it was Wednesday already—only three days till the grand provincial cup contest

As Ann drove her Land Rover to the band room, Martha was miles away in deep thought, imagining sitting in the cornet section near the instrument room. Flashbacks of Chad's blue-faced corpse lying through the doorway made her flesh crawl. How were the musicians expected to blow their hearts out with joy to the world under these circumstances?

'Are you still with me, Martha? You've hardly said a thing since we left home,' said Ann, squinting at her, concerned by her friend's sad state.

Martha pulled herself together for Ann's sake.

When they arrived, the two women spent the next few hours running through the instrument list, when Martha spotted something missing.

'Look—there should be two euphoniums in stock, but there's only one.'

Ann took the list from her for a closer look. 'Which band members play that instrument?'

'There's Mel who has one on loan and whom I can't imagine wanting to steal. She appears too fragile to take on a tall hulk as Chad. Then there's Victor whom I don't know that well, and I can't see why he would need to do that—he has his own instrument.'

'That doesn't mean he's the assailant, but the police will have to investigate that. When we've finished here, would you mind making a copy of that list that shows one missing? I'll give it to Isaac.'

When they'd finished in the instrument room, they headed towards the kitchen.

'I'm glad to get away from that creepy room. I'm sure I could still see bloodstains in the wood. It puts my teeth on edge.'

'Let's make a cup of tea and eat our sandwiches while we talk to Matt,' said Ann, seeing him poke his head out of the kitchen.

'I'm glad he said to meet here,' said Martha. 'We've no days left to deal with all this between now and Saturday.'

'I've put the urn on for you ladies, but I won't be staying after our meeting.'

'Thanks so much, Matt,' said Martha, following him into the kitchen.

'Mind if we make ourselves a cup of tea to have with our lunch?' Ann asked Matt. 'Would you like tea or coffee?'

'No, thanks. I had an early lunch before I left. Shall we go into the secretary's office to talk? It's out of the way in case anyone arrives early,' said Matt. 'I'll wait in there for you.'

The ladies made themselves a drink, and Ann joined Matt in the office. Martha snipped the lock on the front door and then carried the sandwiches and tea on a tray and joined them.

'We are here on behalf of Detective Inspector Isaac Yules to gather information about the movement of band members between our band and the Junior Band,' said Martha,' trying to sound confident.

'What kind of movement do you mean?' Matt asked warily.

Ann glanced at Martha and then back at Matt. 'We need to find out if other band members can access keys to the door of the band hall. Only a few people have a key, and your security has been breached somehow,' said Ann.

'I'm the only one with a key from the Junior Band. Bob lives nearby, and if I misplace it, I can always give him a call. I was going to ask him to get us duplicate, as it's rather a nuisance having to do that. Before the old hall burnt down, several people held them.'

'We deliberately restricted access when we suspected shenanigans were going on after I was locked in the music library,' said Martha.

'Oh, yes—Andre had told me about that.'

'And we've just discovered a euphonium has gone missing after we completed an inventory.'

'Mmm—that's interesting,' said Matt. 'Only Victor and Mel play that instrument. Although we don't have euphonium players in our Junior Band, Victor helps out with teaching music when he can.'

Ann opened her dossier and picked up her pen. 'Matt—do you have a record of the musicians from Martha's band who have been helping the juniors? We need to find out when they were in the band room.'

'Funny you should say that. Normally I wouldn't keep a record, but after Andre told me about the mischief that had taken place and that people were accusing the youths, I started noting down who accessed the band room the days the Junior Band were using it.'

Ann's eyes glowed suddenly. 'You mean you've documented names and dates? That's wonderful—just what we're looking for.'

'So, you think that one of those players is the culprit?' he asked, his forehead wrinkling.

'No, I'm not saying that at all. But we need to determine whether someone entered the building alone to perform a misdeed.'

Ann and Martha spoke at length about the details of the malicious attacks to see if Matt could identify any adults assisting the juniors who could have acted covertly in a crowded room.

'Let me see … four of your musicians join us regularly on Tuesdays and Saturdays—Ernie, Victor, Susan and Les, and if you want my opinion, I can't recall anything suspicious about any of them.'

Ann had been busy jotting down the names as he spoke, while Martha leaned over her shoulder squinting as she craned her neck to read the names.

'Yes, I know what you mean, Matt,' said Martha. They are good people and valued players. It's hard to imagine that one of them could be capable of … of murder.'

Ann glanced at her wristwatch. 'Matt, is there anything you can remember that happened at the practices during the past month that bewildered you?'

'I'm not sure what you mean, but I'm trying to think about recent practices,' he said, twiddling his fingers on the office desk.

'There is something—or maybe nothing at all. Just an incident that happened and I've since been wondering if I should have mentioned it—then, of course, I thought I was overreacting.'

Martha sat agaze. 'What is it, Matt—tell us!'

'It's probably nothing, but I mislaid my keys for a short time at one of our practices. I placed them on the kitchen servery, where I always put them during practice. It's such a big bunch, with a key for almost every room. I find them a nuisance in my pockets.'

'What do you mean mislaid them—when was this?' Ann asked.

'Last week ... not Saturday as that was the day of your dress rehearsal. It must have been last Tuesday.'

'That was the day before the podium collapsed and Andre was injured,' blurted Martha. 'What happened to your keys?'

Ann too was bursting for him to get to the point as she noted everything down.

'I always leave them in the same place in the corner of the servery and left them there while I organised my music scores on the podium. I remember someone said we'd run out of milk. Only a few of the youths partake in tea or coffee, but the people from your band usually like a cup at half-break.'

'Oh, yes. That's why we get a bit extra on a Monday, so there's enough for you people on Tuesday—carry on,' said Martha.

'As I remember, Victor called out to me that he would whip up to the diary and get some milk. I was busy sorting out my music, and it wasn't anything that would cause me to be suspicious.'

'Are you saying there was a window of opportunity for Victor or someone else to take the keys? But they couldn't do anything with them while they were at practice, could they? They'd have to take them the following day to get a key cut,' said Martha, jumping ahead of him.

'No, wait. I think there may have been a moment—an opportunity for Victor or anyone else to go to the village and get a key cut somewhere,' said Ann.

Martha's mouth gaped.

Matt slumped on the desk, looking glum. 'That's what I've been wondering—it has played on my mind since Andre fell from the podium. Victor just seems so plausible as though butter wouldn't melt in his mouth.'

'Hang on—you didn't tell me when you'd noticed the keys had gone,' said Ann.

'Oh, sorry—I saw they'd been moved, but I couldn't locate them. After I'd sorted my music on the podium, I saw the urn was steaming and went to turn it down. As I walked into the kitchen, I saw that my keys weren't where I left them. I asked the band if anyone had moved them, but they hadn't. I forgot to ask Victor when he returned with the milk because by then, we were already playing.'

Martha glanced at her wristwatch. 'We must finish here soon before the members arrive.'

'When did the keys turn up?' Ann asked, determined to extract every detail from him.'

'At half-break, I went to the kitchen to search for them and found them on the opposite side of the servery where I'd left them. It baffled me, and I wondered if I was overworked and having memory lapses. But ever since then, I haven't stopped thinking someone may have moved them deliberately. I gathered it must have been one of the youths shifting them to annoy me, and even if they had, no one would own up to the prank.'

Ann nodded her head as she continued writing and then looked up. 'So, there was ample opportunity for someone to slip out and get a key cut while you were standing at the podium. Apart from Victor, others could have hopped in their car and zipped up to the village. Did you notice anyone else leave the band room that day?'

'Look—once I'm on that podium, I notice nothing except the scores in front of me and the music or bad notes I hear from the players. There can often be people scurrying off to the music library to copy sheets of music or to the bathroom. Perhaps I just absentmindedly misplaced the keys and shifted them myself.'

'I'll visit the local hardware shop which cuts keys—I've seen their billboard outside the shop. I'll see if they have any evidence that someone brought one of the band room keys in to be cut Tuesday a week ago. Can I borrow your key, Matt, just for today? I'll drop back to you after practice later.'

'Sure, of course,' he said, unfastening the key from the bunch. 'I'd be keen to find out.'

"I'll ask them for a copy of the invoice as proof.'

Martha shuddered, gritting her teeth. 'This is getting creepier by the minute. To think that all this is happening in a little country brass band like ours.'

'It's in places like this that creepy things do happen I'm afraid, Martha.'

We'd better get out of here. Some people have arrived—and there's Winnie. Thanks for meeting us, Matt. Let's not say a word to anyone about our conversation, please,' said Martha.

'I'll see you later, Matt,' said Ann. 'I'll pop your key back to you later today.'

'Thanks, Ann. Take care, ladies. Let's keep each other informed, shall we?'

'We will,' said Martha, walking off to the kitchen with Ann in tow, as Matt waved and left the band room.

Winnie hurried into the kitchen. 'Hi, girls, what was Matt doing here? Picking up some music I'll bet.'

'He was looking for something he'd mislaid. I think he found it,' said Martha, who wasn't a good liar but could fob Winnie off sufficiently.

When Andre arrived, he asked to speak to Ann alone in his office before the practice began.

'I hate to put this on you without warning, but you did so well in saving us at the dress rehearsal recording standing in for Errol, I have to ask you to do that again, except this time, for Chad.'

Ann's eyes boggled. The upshot of what he just said came as a shock asking her to replace their virtuoso principal cornet player, the champion of champions in the whole province. Martha had told her it was through Chad's open solo that the Brassholes had gained enough points to win the cup. That was the tipping point. Since then the Haversham Hooters have been desperate to win the cup back again.

'But there's no time for me to prepare and I didn't pack my cornet to take to Martha's. I had no idea I'd be staying so long.'

'We can take care of that—just as we did when you stood in for Errol, and how beautifully you played that day. I couldn't fault your performance at all—I'm sure you could tackle it. He was playing *You Raise Me Up*. For somebody of your calibre, that would be a cakewalk.'

'I know that piece well. Perhaps I could help you out. I just hope I'll make the grade on Saturday though.'

'From what I've heard through the grapevine, you would be well up to the mark.'

Ann knew that Andre was desperate and was just trying to humour her, but she didn't want to let him down. She was aware they had no replacement for Chad, and the band had been knocked about lately, not only by his death but the interruption to several of their rehearsals by the other attacks. They needed a boost.

'Alright then, I'll do it. I can't guarantee I can get enough practice in by then, but I'll do my best.'

Andre's face beamed, and for the first time in weeks, his demeanour changed to his previous cheery disposition. He now had a spring in his step as they left the office to join the rest of the band who were seated, waiting for him.

'I'll arrange for Len to open the instrument room. I've given him a key until we sort out who will be the new custodian. I'll ask him to arrange for you to take home a cornet which you'll have to sign it out.'

'I could have brought my instrument from home, but I didn't think to pack it when I came to stay with Martha.'

'Look—if you don't mind, seeing we have lost our lead cornet, I was wondering if you would oblige for the rest of the contest?' Andre implored.'

'I ... well, I suppose I can't leave you in the lurch at this stage ... oh, alright.'

Andre's face lit up like a Christmas tree.

'What's this I hear,' said Martha, joining the conversation. 'Something about you playing the cornet?'

'Guess what Andre has asked me to do,' said Ann.

'You aren't playing for us at the contest, are you? I wondered if he might ask you to do that. Are you filling Chad's boots? That's a brave feat not to be envied, but I know you can do it. You'll have to do some practise and leave solving the crime to that cute, young Isaac, the detective.'

'Not if I can help it—I've worked hard at getting to this point and won't throw the towel in yet.'

Martha gave her a half-smile, knowing what pressure she was under already.

You can use a cornet from the storeroom. It's so exciting.'

'Yes, I know, Len's going to organise that—we'd better get to our seats, Martha— Andre is about to start.'

Chapter Twenty-two

He's All Keyed-Up!

Ann dropped Martha at the gate and then headed off to drop the key off to Matt. He lived a few miles down the road from Martha's house, and as she drove there, her shoulders couldn't have dropped much further forward. Her bottom lip always jutted out when glum and the corners of her mouth turned down. 'Darn, darn and darn!' she roared, banging both hands on the steering wheel. 'So close and yet so far away!'

She stepped out of the vehicle, hoping Matt hadn't heard her ranting through the closed window of her car.

'Hi, Ann,' he chirped, greeting her with a smile of hopeful expectation. 'How did you get on?'

She stopped on the path to his house, almost in tears of frustration. 'No good, Matt. I can't believe a hardware shop like that doesn't keep records of what keys they cut. They have an account of purchases and transactions for that day, but it could have been any of them. No proof that your key has been duplicated. All is lost because of their poor record keeping!'

Matt looked at Ann's wrought face with empathy.

'The shopkeeper said that a man came rushing through the door last week all keyed-up handing him a bunch of keys—some idiot he said, who swore like a trouper saying that his wife had lost her hers again and could he have this lot cut asap. Cost him a packet!!! he told me.'

'That's disappointing, Ann, but you were on the right track. Maybe we can narrow it down to the four men from your band who were there that day, except that some of our youths are university students who drive to practice in their daddy's cars or have one of their own. It could have been any of them.'

'This is getting out of hand. Poor Martha—she'll be thinking they must change the lock again, but it has only just been done. Perhaps it's time to get a code or PIN. That will put the kibosh on everything,' said Ann.

'I'm sure we'll get to the bottom of it. I'll try to piece it all together again and see what I can come up with.'

'Thanks for the loan of the key, Matt, and your support. Whoever it is has got us flummoxed. But people like that eventually get themselves into a corner. Let's just hope the band can still perform well at the contest on Saturday. I feel so sorry for them all.'

'They'll pull through. They weathered the storm when the old band room burnt down, and they are a determined lot. Ah yes—I forgot to say that Detective Yule rang to say he is dropping by tomorrow. He too is trying to narrow it down, and he and his associate will also interview band members.'

'That's okay, we're working together on this, but we both have unique approaches.'

'Excuse the cliché, but many hands make light work, and the sooner we find the mongrel, the better.'

'Well, I'll get off now. Thanks for everything. I'll keep in touch,' said Ann, stepping into her vehicle.

♫ ♫ ♫

As Ann trudged up the garden path to Martha's front door with a glum expression on her face, she immediately perked up when a strong whiff of beef stew wafted through the front door. Scout rushed up almost bowling her over with glee.

'Something smells tasty,' she said to Martha as she bent down to greet her four-legged friend.

'I've already fed him. It's you I'm concerned about,' Martha said at the sight of Ann's downcast face.

'How on earth did you rustle up a meal that fast? You haven't been home long since I dropped you off.'

'Oh—you didn't notice I put the slow-cooker on this morning before we went out. The beef is from the farmer across the road, and the herbs and vegetables are from my garden. You look as though the world has ended. I'll put the kettle on.'

A short while later, they sat at the dining table, enjoying Martha's stew discussing the day's events.

'I'm sorry to hear about the hardware shop. I suppose if it were a proper locksmith, they would have kept proper records. Do you still think it could have been one of our players at Junior Band—or your people who help at our practices?'

'I don't know—we can't surmise anything. There was a window of opportunity when Matt left his keys lying around.'

'Well, I've got another theory if that's the case. There are four members in possession of a key who live with someone. Any of the residents living with them could have had access to the key. You and I are excluded, but others could have duplicated the key for whatever reason.'

'So, you thought of that possibility too. I was going to bring that up with you tonight. Great minds think alike,' Ann said, with a warm smile. 'I haven't documented their home profiles yet. I will do that when I visit each one individually.'

'That would mean your investigation would need to extend to them, and that's a considerable amount of people.'

'Would you mind giving me a rundown of who they are after we finish our meal?' I'll have to check them all out while I'm looking for people with a motive.'

'Yes, sure—as long as my memory serves me well.'

After eating, they cleared away the dishes and sat back at the table—Ann with her dossier in hand. Martha popped the top off a bottle of her home-brewed ginger beer and offered a glass to Ann.

'You haven't lost your touch. Perhaps you can show me how to make this stuff before I return home. Now—shall we start with Bob?'

'I hate even to go there, but even beloved Bob and his wife have their daughter and son-in-law living with them. Neither of them is a musician.'

She reached for her glass of ginger beer.

'And then there's Andre whose mother recently moved in with him and his wife. I doubt if there's a motive there. Matt lives with his wife and small children. His wife is a darling and is a pillar of our community involved in charity work.'

There was a long list for Martha to go through and it took the two women the rest of the evening to compile a summary of each one. Ann placed a question mark against the name if there could be room for a motive.

That night as she sat up in bed with a cup of hot milk and her dossier on her lap, for the first time, she was overwhelmed. Perhaps she should have stuck to the private investigating of unfaithful spouses. That's how she began her business until she became bored and wanted to return to *the real thing*.

Her eyes smarted with strain as she fought off brain fatigue. Although many family members could take and duplicate the key, there was one who felt threatened by the Riverlea Brassholes. Who could it be?

First, an arsonist burned the original band hall and now all these current malicious happenings. They would indicate they had a vendetta against the whole band as an entity and not an individual. It didn't make sense.

Ann finished her milk and sighed, thinking that the upcoming contest on Saturday held up the progress of her enquiries. She felt heartless pressurising the members to answer multiple questions during an already traumatic time following Chad's death. The contest couldn't come quick enough. Once they got that out of the way, she and Martha would be free to centre their attention on solving this horrendous crime.

'Are you still awake in there?' Martha called, tapping lightly on her door. 'I need to discuss your plans for tomorrow.'

'Yes, I'm still awake—come on in.'

When Martha opened the door, Scout craned his neck to greet her by licking her hand.

'Get back on your bed—lie down, boy.'

'I don't mind—he just wants to say goodnight,' said Martha.

'Being an ex-police dog, he knows not to lick people to death, but now he's retired, I do get tempted to relax the rules. Now—about tomorrow.'

'You said that you plan to call on some of the band members, but to be perfectly honest, I think it would be … well … difficult to achieve two days before the contest.'

'Come right out with it, Martha—you mean it would be intrusive at such a crucial time.'

'It's a catch-22 predicament. I know it's of prime urgency to catch the criminal now before they disappear. On the other hand, it seems insensitive to barge in and start interrogating them two days before the biggest deal of the year for them.'

'That, dear Martha is what I've been in a quandary about all evening—to do or not to do. I'm between a rock and a hard place for sure.'

Just as she finished talking, a loud noise emerged from the floor next to the bed.

''Oh, my goodness—is that Scout snoring? I've never heard a dog snore like that before.'

This sudden interruption caused them both to burst out laughing.

'Time for bed—I'm all done for the night,' said Martha, picking up Ann's cup to take to the kitchen.

'Wait—I think you're right. Two more days won't matter, and after the contest, it'll be full steam ahead. You've given me plenty to go on with which I can mull over to see if there's any hint of a red herring amongst your troupe.'

Chapter Twenty-three

Ann was in the backyard the next morning throwing a ball to Scout when her cell phone sounded. Isaac rang to say that he was with the police who had searched for the murder weapon in the field and bushes surrounding the band hall since dawn with negative results.

'They are going to drain the creek between the building and Tom's orchard,' said Isaac.

'How long will that take?' asked Ann.

'They'll be out of there by the end of the day.'

For the rest of Thursday, Ann spent most of the day practising her solo, *You Raise Me Up* and some of the trickier pieces that Chad had played so well.

Martha received a phone call from Tom to say he could hear the angelic melody from where he sat, and it was a winner. He also said to tell Ann that the police were all over his property and some young detective told him they were going to drain the creek later in the day.

It was difficult for Ann to focus on the criminal case at hand and the preparation for the contest, but in either situation, she didn't want to let Martha down by giving up.

♪ ♪ ♪

Friday couldn't come soon enough, and the afternoon practice was the last rehearsal before the *big day*. For some reason, the culprit had ceased attacking the band since Chad's death, but they had already done sufficient damage to knock the stuffing out of most of the players and undermine their confidence.

When the practice was over, Martha had the go-ahead from Andre to give a small announcement after he had made his.

'Seeing this is a one-day event which we are hosting here in this building, we will have to provide food for the day for which the committee has already budgeted. It's a wonder any of them would want to come with Chad's death treated as suspicious and now all over the news.'

'Who's taking care of the food? Is the committee buying it?' Len asked Martha.

'No, Andre has arranged for some of your wives to order finger food from the local bakery and pizzeria, and several women will bake scones for afternoon tea. He said he also hoped that some of our bandswomen could assist in the food department.'

Martha shook her head and stalked off following her announcement, irritated by the attitude of male egotism in brass bands treating women as second-class citizens. Nothing had changed since she had first started playing during her youth.

'Come on, let's get out of here,' before you and I are asked to bake scones too,' she said, tugging on Ann's sleeve. 'He seems oblivious to the fact that we women in the band also put in hours of practice each week, all ten of us.'

Ann was glad to be away from the band hall and on their way back home. 'I'm all done in today.'

'You know, Ann ... while I sat there playing near the spot where Chad ... you know what—I glanced around the room at every single person and tried to visualise each one as a killer,' said Martha, as Ann pulled out onto the main road. 'I just couldn't see any of them fit the profile of a murderer, not one.'

'That's just the perfect example of how a criminal or psychopath operates. A calculated killer will cunningly fit into a group or community and go about their business like one of the lads,' said Ann. 'They will keep a low profile under the radar, so they end up being the last one anyone would suspect. It could even be a woman. And the police haven't confirmed what the murder weapon was, although they know it was a blunt instrument, excuse the pun.'

'Mmm, I suppose if you put it like that, it could well be any of them. This could be a hard case to crack, don't you think?'

'I do—it has been enough to keep me awake nights, and that's unusual for me, even with the most complicated of cases. But we have God on our side. You'll see we are going to crack it. But after you win the contest—right?'

'Yes—after we win the Sylvester Cup!'

Chapter Twenty-four

The Big Day

The morning of the contest Martha had the jitters. She woke early, even before the rooster crowed and busied herself in her music room packing up her folders and instrument ready to take to the hall. Although the contest didn't start until 10 am, they had a heap of things to do.

Martha sat down to the table as it was Ann's turn to prepare their breakfast, but this time neither of them had much of an appetite, and they sat drinking coffee and eating toast with Martha's quince jelly. 'Shall we get there early just to make sure everything is in place?' she asked.

'I think you should let go and allow the members who offered to handle the preparations to carry out their duties. Bob and his wife are setting things up along with Winnie's husband and Andre's son, that tall, strapping lad who is going be there, he told me.'

'But I usually get there early to organise things. I've been doing it for decades,' Martha murmured.

'Many people are going to be assisting, and you are competing today. I don't know how you can keep up with it all. Perhaps it's time to let some of the others pull their weight.'

Martha stood up and combed her fingers through her hair. 'You're right. I think my involvement with the band had always helped to take the focus off my loneliness after Frank died. I kept so active I didn't have time to feel sorry for myself, but it is getting too much for me—the music library, the kitchen and competing.'

'Why don't you have a roster for the kitchen? Surely that task is everyone's responsibility. The same as for the cleaning as I hear you do the bathrooms too.'

'Bob sweeps the floors each week, and he and some of the men do the lawn. But you're right—it's time to get some rosters going. I'll see to it after the contest.'

On the Friday before they went home, Andre informed them that the coroner would release Chad's body to his relatives after the weekend, as the funeral was scheduled for the following Wednesday.

♫ ♫ ♫

Bob had already opened the hall, and the car park was filling up fast as Ann drove in with her Land

Rover. Tom stood by the gate grinning from ear to ear dressed in his finest, ushering people into the car park. He had made an excellent job of painting a placard which he had fastened to the side gate that led into a large field.

'Fortunately, we've had a dry autumn otherwise we wouldn't have been able to use the field for parking,' said Ann as she pulled up towards the back of the car park. 'And I don't fancy traipsing across lumpy grass carrying our music gear, so I'm glad there are still a few parking spaces left.'

'Me too. Our old band room had a much larger car park, but the building was small. Can't have it both ways, I suppose.'

As the women started taking their instruments and music folders out of the boot of the car, Ann's cell phone rang.

'Oh dear, I must turn the thing off before I go inside,' she said as she took the call and waved her hand at Martha to indicate to go ahead inside.

It was Isaac with some more news for her, and this time it sounded promising.

'We think we may have found the murder weapon in the creek after we drained it on Thursday, and forensics are testing it.'

'That's wonderful news—mind if I call you back after the band contest—I'm there now. I really have to go.'

Ann ended the call and hurried into the band room where a crowd of people sat in the auditorium. She cringed as Martha met her at the door but was impressed with how organised they were for a small country band as she glanced at all the people.

Ann followed Martha into the change room where they both applied their make-up and did a last-minute check of their appearance.

'The uniform looks great on you. Good thing you packed your black trousers when you came to stay with me. They don't provide them, unfortunately. Take your instrument and music folder to the secretary's office. It's soundproof, and that's where our band can leave their instruments and have a warm-up if we want. I'll meet you there, and then we can find a seat. The other bands are using the large room at the back of the stage. It's soundproofed too.'

Ann picked up her gear and wandered off to the office to unload her kit when she heard over the speaker that the first band was about to start. Half of the band members were chatting away to each other or warming up and checking their instruments and music.

Martha put her things inside the door. 'I can see some of our band are seated over there at the left. Let's join them, and I'll show you my program. We must make sure we don't miss our call.'

Ann followed Martha over to the row of seats where her colleagues were sitting. After they joined them, Martha showed her the itinerary. 'Here we are—we're second on the list, and then we stop for lunch. Only four bands are competing, and Haversham Hooters is last. Remember I said they are the band who had kept the cup for decades until we took it off them last year.'

'Oh, yes, I remember. That would have given them a shake-up.'

'You can say that again—several of them were bitter.'

'So, what time are the solos—when am I on?'

'You're first, directly after lunch. The duets are after the solos. Errol is here, thank God—otherwise, Andre would have dropped you in it again and asked you to oblige.'

Ann grimaced. 'I don't think so—the solo will take it out of me, so no chance of me doing that.'

'Shhh—they're about to start. Richmond Brass is playing first.'

Ann couldn't hold her focus on the band that had played on stage. Her mind was preoccupied with the phone call she'd received from Isaac about the murder weapon. Would they have thrown it in the creek—and what would they have used to cause a dent in Chad's skull?' She glanced over at the two rows of players from Martha's band sitting in front of them, and her mind played games with her, as she tried to imagine each person bringing a blunt instrument down with full force on the skull of a fellow bandsman.

The applause from the audience rocketed her back to reality, as Martha's elbow jibed her ribs.

'We're next. The compere will give a spiel for about ten minutes while we're getting ready—all set?'

'As ready as I'll ever be.'

Ann was bursting to tell Martha about Isaac's news, but she'd agreed with herself that today of all days she would not let that evil deed or anything to do with it upset Martha or any of the band members on their special day.

They headed off back to the office to fetch their instruments and folders and then stood back in the hall lining the wall like the rest of the band waiting for the last call.

Chapter Twenty-five

Andre lifted his baton as the players raised their instruments simultaneously in readiness to begin the *Glenn Miller Medley*. They started with *Chattanooga Choo Choo*, and Will, who had completely recovered from his burns, proudly stood up on the stage to perform the solo part on his trombone. As he blew into his instrument, his face went the colour of a tomato, not from blowing too hard, but from being unable to get a note out. He apologised and looked down the bell of his trombone and then blew again. Flummoxed, he turned to his fellow trombonists and shrugged.

'I don't know what's happening—it was fine when I warmed up in the office.'

The adjudicators waited patiently and asked if he wished to continue, or would he need a few moments to sort it out?

'Here, said Bill, the trombonist who played the second part. Use my instrument for the solo. There are enough of us to cover you.'

'Gee whiz, thanks. This is so weird, though.'

Bill stood down while Will took the floor and played like a champion.

After the applause had stopped and they were given the nod to leave their seats, they gathered backstage. Will inspected his trombone and couldn't see what had caused the problem. Ann, seeing he was in trouble, approached him, as she smelled a rat. 'Let me look, Will,' she said, reaching for the instrument. She put her hand inside the bell of the trombone, straining to push her fingers inside. 'Voila! Here is the offender,' she blurted, extracting a long scarf from the bell of the trombone. Will went white with shock. This time he took it as a personal attack.

'Right! I'm off to talk to the adjudicators now! This is another case of sabotage,' Andre ranted. 'Come on, you lot. You all did exceptionally well. Get some refreshments—there's a good spread out there for your lunch. I'm off to make sure we haven't been unfairly disadvantaged,' he raved, as he stormed off the stage.

'Let's go, Ann. You'd better get your lunch and then check your instrument,' said Martha. 'We can't be too careful now, as it looks like our psycho is on the prowl again.'

♫ ♫ ♫

It had been at least a decade since Ann had stood on stage in front of an auditorium full of strangers to play a solo.

The rest of the band sat in the audience with eyes fixated on her. She took her place next to the microphone placing her music sheet on the stand while Len's wife, Petra, the pianist, made a bow as she walked over to the piano and sat down.

The auditorium went silent, while Ann waited for Petra to play the introduction, and when she held up her cornet to play, one could hear a pin drop as she gave a breath-taking performance of *You Raise Me Up*. Andre's mouth fell wide open, mesmerised with tears in his eyes, and then she brought the house down with a standing ovation.

Martha rushed up as Ann stepped off the stage and threw her arms around her, and as she took her seat, she spotted Victor stomping out of the auditorium

'My goodness, I think I can safely say that even Chad, God rest his soul wouldn't have performed like that—it was amazing,' blurted Martha to Ann who had sat down next to her. 'Now we just need to see how the next three go, as there are four of you competing. Haversham Hooters have entered every section too.'

'What time is the last event?'

'It goes until 5 pm. After the solos, three bands are competing in the duets, including ours. It's a long day. At least you can relax—now it's my turn.'

The women sat through the rest of the solo section exchanging opinions on the skill of each player. Martha found them no comparison to Ann, but she realised that band contests can be fickle and not always turn out how one would expect.

After the last soloist walked down the stairs, Ann tugged on Martha's arm. 'You'd better go and get ready—our band is on soon.'

'Thanks—we are number three on the list—so Errol and I have time to warm up. At least the office is soundproofed.'

Ann left Martha to find Errol and went outside to stretch her legs. While she was out there, a few players from Riverlea Brassholes approached her to say what an outstanding performance she gave and asked how she had become such a virtuoso. Although she tried to be sociable and engage in light banter, her mind kept mulling over the possibility of one of them being a killer. It was an unnerving situation to be in, but Martha and Andre would also be putting on a brave face for the rest of the band.

'Coming inside?' Andre called from the front door of the building. 'We are on—it's time for us to play *Pie Jesu*. You'd better go and warn Martha and Errol.'

Ann saw Martha scurrying along towards them with Errol in tow ready to join the band as they were about to go on stage.

'Just think how proud Frank would be right now. Let's go and win that cup for him, Martha,' Ann said, warmly, knowing how much it meant to her to carry on his heritage.

'Say a prayer for me, please. I'm shaking like a leaf—not confident like you.'

'I've already prayed—now you just go for it!'

The auditorium went quiet again as the band stepped onto the stage with Martha and Errol going forward to the front and Andre in readiness to conduct. Ann gave Martha a thumbs-up from her seat in the front row cornet section.

The compere announced the piece of music, *Pie Jesu*, which was an *open concert selection.*

With the band softly giving backing support, Martha and Errol stood ready to play the duet in two parts—Errol playing the soprano and Martha on B flat cornet.

Before they began, Errol suddenly unbuttoned his jacket, throwing it aside. He scratched his arms like a madman and then clawed at his chest frantically, his face turning bright red with beads of sweat running down his forehead. Martha had never seen him like that—it couldn't have been nerves as he was always so calm.

'Sorry,' he said to Martha. There is something in my jacket. It wasn't there before today—I left it hanging in the men's change room while we were warming up our instruments in the office.'

Andre spotted the trouble. He crept behind Ann's row and tapped her on the shoulder from behind.

'Please—help us. Rescue Errol—you can do it. There's a fly in the ointment somewhere again. Please, Ann, otherwise we're finished.'

Ann took one look at the grim expression on Andre's face and rushed forward to save Errol whispering in his ear that she would play for him. Errol handed her his cornet and hurried backstage behind the curtain, still scratching himself.

'We can do it,' Ann said to Martha. 'Just remember what we did at the dress rehearsal,' she said and quieted herself taking long, deep breaths. Martha waved to the adjudicators that they were ready.

Just as the pair had surprised everyone on the day of the dress rehearsal, they did it again—and once more, Ann had saved the day. They both gave an outstanding recital that rocked the whole audience.

At the end of their performance, Martha rushed backstage to Errol and brought him his jacket which he'd hurled on the floor.

'Drop it!' he blurted, still standing behind the curtains. Someone has interfered with it somehow. They have infested it with fleas or something.'

'Let me see,' said Martha, holding the jacket open by the buttons. 'I can't see anything. Perhaps we should let Ann inspect it. She's an expert.'

'Well, that woman rescued me—remarkable, she is. I need to find her and say thanks.'

During the rest of the contest Martha, Ann and Errol met with Andre to describe what happened.

'I think I know what caused the itchiness—age-old itchy powder. They use it at parties for pranks, except this was not at all funny,' said Ann.

Andre went straight back to the adjudicators to let them know that someone had tried again to sabotage the Riverlea Brassholes' chances of winning again.

Chapter Twenty-six

The Sylvester Cup

The adjudicators heard Andre out mercifully letting Errol off for making a spectacle of himself by throwing his jacket on the floor—and Ann for standing in for him to do the duet with Martha. They judged Ann on her merits as any other player, despite the disturbance the commotion had caused.

At half-time during the afternoon break, Ann sensed animosity as members of the Hooters stood eyeballing her.

She and Martha took their finger food and coffees out to the front steps to get some fresh air.

'While the compere was introducing us on stage before we played our first piece, I noted some ugly glares from a few of your rivals. It almost put me off playing,' Ann said softly, looking over her shoulder.

'I know exactly what you mean. I saw it too.'

'And what's wrong with our man, Victor over there. He looks down in the mouth about something,' said Ann, throwing her head sideways in the direction of the euphonium player leaning against a wall. 'He's just watching people and not engaging with anyone,' Ann said, lifting her thumb in the kitchen's direction.

'I don't know—he's an excellent player, but he tends to keep to himself most of the time. I don't think he's a happy person,' said Martha, discreetly trying to glance over her shoulder to watch him.

'That Haversham lot seem quite resentful—not good sports, I'd say,' said Ann, reacting to some of the dark glances she caught as a handful of their players walked past her to go back inside the hall.

'You can say that again—they loathe us for taking the cup last year. Imagine if we won it again.'

'Come on, Martha. Only two more duets and then they'll announce the winners after a short break. Not long to go now, and then we can get back to solving the case.'

It seemed forever for Ann to sit through the rest of the duets as she struggled to stop her mind going off on tangents, trying to solve the murder case.

After a brief interlude and bathroom break, Martha couldn't stop the butterflies flitting around in her stomach when she caught sight of the adjudicators walking onto the stage seating themselves in a row across the front of the podium. The compere carried the notable, brass Sylvester Cup which gleamed under the floodlights, and placed it on a small table.

Ann's heart missed a beat. She didn't expect to win, but to get second place would at least give Martha a boost, and she was doing it to help the band, not herself. The clamour of the clapping drowned her thoughts until Martha elbowed her.

'We've done it, we won! The cup's ours again—thanks to you bailing us out,' blurted Martha, tears streaming down her face.

'Really? Fantastic! When do we get to hear the points or to see who won each section?' Ann whispered.

'It's coming now,' Martha replied.

Before the compere invited the Riverlea Brassholes to come onto the stage, he announced the results, and to Ann and Martha's amazement, they had the most points for their performances.

Andre turned in his seat and smiled at them both and then led the whole band onto the stage. As they walked up the steps and stood under the lights, there was a loud commotion that filled the room, with flashes from cameras in the audience blinding them. As the musicians took their seats, Martha caught a glimpse of Victor ducking out backstage. He flew down the stairs through the one-way door that led to the outside carpark. *Perhaps he is ill*, she wondered.

Andre stood as proud as a father with a new-borns baby holding back his emotions as the compere shook his hand and passed him the colossal cup. It was a day that Martha and Ann would never forget.

As the band members gathered with Andre after the contest, he spoke to Martha and handed her the cup.

'We want you to keep hold of this until next year, as we believe you have deserved it with all the effort you have put into our group. Without you, we wouldn't be able to manage, and this is a token of our appreciation. You have done us all proud and Frank would be too if he were here.'

Chapter Twenty-Seven

That evening after the contest, Ann lay back soaking in the hot bath, letting the tension of the past week slowly dissipate. The contest had drained her, despite winning her solo. Saving the band twice over was an honourable feat, but that wasn't her purpose for staying away from her own home for so long. She missed her quaint cottage by the sea and her relatively sedate life walking her dog along the promenade. Her private investigation service was mild compared to what she had been exposed to with the Riverlea Brassholes the past month.

She had told Martha that the police found the murder weapon and tomorrow she would go to the station to collect it and start her investigations following the forensic report.

As she lay revelling in the heat of the water swirling around her neck, she struggled to stay awake. It was time to climb out and get to bed, and her brain needed to rejuvenate in readiness for the challenging task of finding Chad's killer. A good sleep would do precisely that.

♫ ♫ ♫

You must excuse me,' said Martha, still in her dressing gown the next morning. I'm usually up and dressed by now, but I'm exhausted.'

'I know what you mean,' said Ann, who was already dressed and bouncing about, eager to get along to the police station. 'I was shattered last night, but a long hot bath did the trick and took away all the aches from the tension that had accumulated. We've had a hard month, and it's not over yet.'

'Are you off somewhere today?'

'Isaac asked me to check out the object they found in the creek to help identify whether it could be the murder weapon.'

'Poor you, not being able to take it easy. I'm chilling out today to spend time with my animals.'

'Let me know if you need anything—I'll pass the supermarket on the way.'

'Thanks, but I'm all stocked up. If I think of anything, I'll phone you.'

Ann picked up her document satchel and headed out the door. Adrenaline began winding its way through her veins as she pushed her foot down on the gas pedal until an in-your-face speed sign pulled her foot off the pedal. *Darn, it's too difficult to keep the vehicle at 50 kph.*

The frustration of driving on narrow, country roads vexed her, but the trip to the small, provincial station was short.

The young police officer glanced at her sideways as she scurried in through the door, flashing her security card at the officer on the desk. Her clothes were almost retro, as she hated keeping up with current trends.

After meeting with Ann in his office, Isaac took her to the forensic exhibit vault to show her the murder weapon.

'Here it is,' he said, holding up a plastic bag revealing the 12-inch crescent wrench.

'See the markings on here,' he said, rubbing his finger over the surface of the tool's head. 'This, we believe, has caused the tiny fractures and indentations in Chad's skull. The patterns match perfectly.'

Even though Ann had experienced years of dealing with gruesome forensic reports and sighting mangled bodies, this sent a shiver down her spine at the thought of Chad with his head bashed in.

'I've just had a thought. Looking at this reminded me of another spanner I've seen recently just like this. I'm sure it looks like the one that Jim, our horn player pulled out of our copier machine. We think someone must have jammed it deliberately—as I told you—someone who was trying to interfere with the band rehearsals.'

Isaac gave her a disapproving glance. 'You didn't tell me about the copy machine incident.'

Ann quickly thought of an excuse, when the real reason was, she had intended to manage the case herself, privately.

'Oh, I overlooked that one. But I'll contact Jim to arrange to get the spanner off him so we can keep it as an exhibit when this goes to court. Even if it isn't a match, the incident with the copier had to be sabotage, and I believe the crimes are connected.'

'Great stuff, Ann—it's in your hands now. Can I leave you to follow this line of enquiry as well as the rest of the band room vandalism? If you need any help, just call me.'

'Absolutely—I'm right on it and have a few people I'll question in that regard. Thanks, Isaac. I'll be off now if you don't mind.'

Ann couldn't wait to head back to Martha's and show her the spanner. Perhaps she may remember seeing a band member with it.

♫ ♫ ♫

'If only my Frank were still alive—he would recognise that spanner at a glance and know if any of our band members had produced one at any time,' said Martha, pouring Ann a cup of tea. She handed her a raspberry tartlet.

'He was a carpenter, wasn't he? A jolly handy chippie you used to call him. I can recall you saying what a handyman he was in the band room whenever anything needed fixing.'

'He sure was. That's another reason why I miss him so much—he was so practical around the home. Anyway—don't you need to preserve that tool as evidence for the probable court case?'

'They won't use this in court, only the photographs. But they'll keep them in the lockup until the case is closed.'

'When are you going to call around to see Jim and fetch the small spanner, he pulled out of the copier machine?'

'I'll do that today, as I need to compare them as soon as possible. I'll call him after our cup of tea.'

'Scout has been begging for a walk today, but I was tied up on the phone while you were out. Andre phoned to say he and the cornet section are keen to have me as lead cornet and section leader from now on.'

'That's wonderful news—congratulations!'

'He told me he offered the position to you after the concert, but you turned him down, saying that you are returning home when this case his closed. That's a pity as we would make a great team.'

'I'm sorry, Martha, but although I love being here with you and all we enjoy together, I like my own home and little garden. The countryside is beautiful and peaceful, but I miss my beach. I think you would make an excellent team leader and lead cornet player. You've been hiding your light under a bushel.'

Martha's eyes smarted as she soaked up her friend's compliments.

'Thanks, Ann. I appreciate you giving up your life to help me out here. Do you need me to accompany you to visit Jim?'

'No, I'll be fine, but I'd better give him a call first.'

Ann rang Jim as she sat on the veranda in the sun. After she finished, she gave Scout an affectionate rub under his chin. 'I won't be long, boy—I know you're bursting to go to that park at the end of the road. I'll be back soon to take you out,' she said, as the dog whimpered enquiringly.

Ann said goodbye to Martha and dashed down the steps and into her car. Butterflies fluttered inside her stomach as she drove out onto the main road that led to Jim's house. When she arrived, he was out in the front garden at the end of the driveway.

'Come on in. Time for a coffee?'

'I'm fine, thanks, Jim. I just had one with Martha. I wouldn't mind a chat though if you don't mind.'

'Sure, it's still warm enough to sit on the patio. I'll just introduce you to my wife, May before we sit down.'

Jim went inside to the kitchen with Ann in tow where May stood at the bench rolling pastry.

'Oh, hello. Ann—isn't it?' the woman said, rinsing her hands under the tap and drying them. She slipped a cold, moist hand into Ann's.

'I've heard so much about you—only good things.'

Jim interjected. 'If you don't mind, love, Ann can't stay long. She is here to discuss band business, and we'll sit out on the patio.'

'No cup of tea then?' she asked, with a warm smile.

'No, thanks, I've just had one at home.'

Jim brushed the seat he pulled out for Ann and sat opposite her.

'Here is the spanner you wish to inspect. Take it with you if you think it relevant to solving the crime.'

Jim had already taken her advice producing the small spanner in a plastic bag.

'My fingerprints are all over it. What will happen now?'

'That's alright. We know yours will be on it. We'll get it tested and see what others we can find. If the culprit was gloved as they must have been with Chad's murder, I have a plan to follow another trail which I can't disclose to you just now.'

'Well, as long as the cops don't name me as a suspect.'

'I doubt it very much. But I must get off now and get this to the police station. They'll want to photograph it and send it to the lab for testing.'

'Jeepers—it all sounds a bit, *Hercule Poirot!*'

'It is, I suppose—old hat for me, but to a layperson, I expect it sounds rather dramatic.'

'Come—I'll see you to your vehicle,' he said, showing her out the door.

'Bye, May. Sorry, it was such a brief visit,' Ann called, as the woman waved at her from the door.

Ann felt triumphant possessing what she gathered would be a key piece of evidence and couldn't wait to go to the station to match them. She phoned Isaac first to let him know she would be bringing it.

At the station, Isaac already had an evidence photographer waiting to take snaps of the small spanner. Afterwards, he and Ann sat comparing both tools.

'They are a match—it's the same brand, and if you look closer, you can see they both appear to be of the same cast—I'd say no more than four or five years old.'

'That's grand news, but how conclusive is that? Is it a common brand?'

'See this stamp here with small print inside the circle. It's a *Marco* spanner that you'd find at all the mega hardware outlets. They usually sell in sets and are solid, pricey things. It would be hard to find a single tool for sale without the whole collection.'

'That makes it simpler to track. I'll have a sniff around the band and see if any band members can recognise this set.'

A sense of excitement filled Ann's boots as she hurried out to her Land Rover. Isaac had suggested she keep hold of the wrench while tracking the incomplete set. Now she was on a mission—confident that it was the clue to solving the case.

♫ ♫ ♫

Chapter Twenty-eight

Ann had looked forward to sitting at the table over a cup of tea with Martha, trying to check out the clues recorded in her dossier. Now it was time to rack Martha's brains and attempt to isolate one or two people of interest.

'I remember now, where I have seen that spanner set, I hate to say, and it was in the hands of one of our cherished band members,' said Martha tentatively.

'You're not serious—are you sure?'

'Absolutely. Frank had one of those spanners— the middle-sized one, I think, but he never owned the whole set. He must have got it at one of those second-hand tool shops he frequented.'

'So ... what are you trying to say—I don't get it?'

'It's the stamp on the metal. You can't miss it. That's the first thing I noticed when I saw Frank's spanner lying in his workshop. It has a distinctive elephant imprint on the head.'

Ann shook her head. She couldn't grasp what Frank's tools had to do with solving this crime—he had been dead for years.

Martha saw the puzzled look in her face.

'Oh, what I meant to say was that our dear Bob has a full set of those things. Frank even borrowed them from him now and then. But there's no way that he is a killer, and half the band could own a set like that.'

'I understand, Martha. But I'll need to ask Bob to produce his set and see if any are missing. That will be the beginning of this line of enquiry. I'll call him to see if I can visit him tomorrow.'

'Oh dear, poor Bob under scrutiny. There has to be a way we can uncover the real killer.'

'There is the fact that, apart from you, Bob also has keys, along with Andre and Matt. When I dealt with cases like this in the past, the most unlikely small-town and well-loved member of the community often turned out to be a killer.'

'Oh, don't—you just made my skin crawl,' said Martha, shuddering.

'If Bob can show me a full set, I'll cross him off the list.'

'More tea?' Martha asked as she held the teapot over Ann's cup.

'Yes, thanks—this is thirsty work.'

After topping up her cup, Martha sat rubbing her finger across her chin.

'Mmm, there are a few things I think that are questionable and worth investigating—some odd behaviour from one of our band members I've observed lately. Remember you asked me if I've seen any suspicious activity amongst your players? Well, there have been some odd incidences that have concerned me.'

'Great—let's have it, and no holds barred, either,' Ann replied eagerly.

'I've noticed strange antics from Victor lately. He always was a sullen, morose type, but more so during the past month leading up to the concert.'

Ann sat with pen in hand, soaking up the vital information that Martha began to spout forth.

'Do you remember the day of the contest during the half-break when you and I sat on the steps? I mentioned that Victor had a bee in his bonnet about something. He didn't appear to be as happy as the rest of us when we gained the most points that morning, and he was speaking to no one.'

'Yes, I do remember that, but I don't know him as you do.'

'Normally, at practices, he would chat with his colleagues and share a bit of banter, but lately, he has been like a bear with a sore head. That day, he disappeared off the stage when we went up as a full band to receive the cup. When we walked up the steps to take our seats, I caught a glimpse of him suddenly disappearing out the backstage door. It was as if he didn't want to be a party to being awarded the cup.'

'Yes, it sounds like it. And I recall after I played my solo you told me Victor stomped off out of the auditorium,' said Ann.

'Oh—and when the band played the sacred piece, *I'll Walk With God*, he put down his instrument and started fiddling with his valves. I think he has issues with us winning the cup for some reason. You don't think he could have been the saboteur all along, do you?'

'It's possible, Martha, but all this is circumstantial and wouldn't be enough to charge him with anything. He would just say he wasn't well or had to go out to make an urgent call. Of course, if he lied about that, we could always search his phone.'

'Perhaps you could visit his family. I heard that his ex-wife moved to Cambridge. She shares the house with her daughter, Jill.'

'I had already planned to visit them, as I'm still unsure whether Victor managed to cut himself a key somehow. I want to know a bit more about him, but first of all, I'll visit Bob.'

Ann took her teacup back into the kitchen and made the call to the friendly caretaker. He arranged to meet her the next morning, and Ann felt terrible about having to do this, as she had got to know Bob well during her extended stay with Martha, but it had to be done whether he would be embarrassed by it or not.

Chapter Twenty-nine

The next morning during Ann's visit, Bob slammed his toolset down on the table in front of her, his round face red as a strawberry.

Ann felt taken aback at his feisty attitude, as until now, he had always been pleasant and accommodating towards her, and Martha often referred to him as a gentle soul.

'Is everything alright, Dad?' asked his daughter, who poked her head into the dining room to check out the loud bang.'

'We're fine thanks, love. Ann is asking a few questions about that wretched police business at the band.'

Ann had already told Bob she had no time to stop for cups of tea, eager to get as much information as she could from Bob.

He thrust the open toolset in front of her. 'Here you are—see for yourself!'

'Thanks, Bob.' She pulled a pair of rubber gloves from her pocket and removed the spanners from the bag comparing the brand and series, with Bob's tools. They were a perfect match, but Bob's set was complete.

'Well—what did I tell you?' Bob said sharply as she nodded her approval and returned the spanners in her hand to the plastic bag.

'It is the same brand. Thank you, Bob, I appreciate you co-operating with me. It's our only way of finding out if the wrench is a possible murder weapon.'

'Do you know that half the village could have a set like this in their workshops? I think you're on a wild goose chase myself. I'm sorry about my outburst, but I felt as though you were already treating me as a criminal. I suppose you were just doing your job.'

'If you don't mind, I think I will have that cup of tea if it's still on the menu.'

Bob gave her a half-smile. 'Sure, just a moment,' he said as he scurried into the kitchen to ask his daughter to oblige.

'Would you know if any other band members have that same set?'

Bob shook his head. 'No, I haven't seen anyone with one, except Martha's Frank once, but that doesn't mean they don't.'

Ann was keen to get to know a bit more about Bob's daughter and son-in-law and to make sure they had no motive for killing Chad. After an hour of shallow small talk and two cups of tea with macaroons, Ann bustled off to the car half satisfied that Bob was not a person of interest and neither was his family, although they could have had access to his keys.

Driving back to Martha's house, she pondered whether she was following a false lead regarding the spanners—or not. It was clear that someone had damaged the copier with the tool which Jim had extracted and not owned up to it. Perhaps it was an accident, and someone had dropped in the machine while they were trying to repair it. That just leaves the heavy wrench found in the creek, probably discarded there recently—otherwise, it would have shown signs of rust, Ann mused.

It had been a frustrating day for her as she pulled into Martha's driveway, and she could hear Scout whimpering as she walked up to the front door. Martha had taken to keeping him indoors with her as company when Ann went out. Goodness only knows what she is going to do after it's time for her companion to return home.

'You're back, thank the Lord. I don't think I could have held on any longer on tenterhooks wondering what the outcome was,' blurted Martha, as Ann barely had a moment to draw breath and sit down.

'Let me pour us both some of my cider. Don't worry—I haven't added any voltage. I got used to making it without alcohol, as Frank had been on the wagon—sober for years before he passed away.'

Martha pottered around in the kitchen, preparing the drinks while Ann put her dossier in her room. When she returned to the kitchen, Martha had already taken the refreshments out onto the veranda.

Scout almost licked the skin off Ann's hand as she sat at the table. 'Sorry, boy, I couldn't take you this time. How about a run in the park before dinner?'

Scout's ears pricked up while his tail wagged his approval.

It must be great having him as a companion. I know I have Hyacinth, but I can't bring her inside, or have her lie on my bed, save going for a ride with me in my car—we both know what happens with that.'

'Oh, poor Hyacinth,' said Ann. 'She adores you. But I know what you mean—a pig isn't a house pet.'

'Perhaps it's time for me to get a dog, or even a cate—except I don't know how Hyacinth would react,' Martha replied.

'Perhaps Hyacinth and Blossom will be the best of friends—I mean, look at her with Scout. They get on very well.'

'Anyway, come on—I'm bursting to know how you got on with Bob,' said Martha.

'He's in the all-clear as far as the spanner goes—he has the full set, and it's the same brand with all the markings. And I do find it hard to believe that he or his family could have a motive for killing Chad.'

'That's good to know. Even when they didn't like each other and had a few feisty rows, I didn't think he could do it.' said Martha, patting Scout on the head.

'What? I can't remember you telling me they didn't like each and fought. But I suppose that still doesn't mean he would want to kill him.'

'So, what is your plan for your next line of enquiry?' asked Martha.

'Victor Saltman, your euphonium player—he's next. But first I'm going to pay a visit to his ex-wife you said lives with her daughter in Cambridge. I think I'll start my enquiries there. I have an idea.'

'Really—when are you going there? I'll come along with you.'

'Yes, that would be good. But first I need to make sure the information you gave me is correct—such as her name and address.'

'I don't have her address, sorry. How will you track her down?'

'Isaac is doing a record search. He phoned me this morning, and I asked him to look up all the details of Victor's ex-wife and her whereabouts.'

'He will be livid when he finds out you've been snooping around his ex-wife.'

'I know—perhaps I need to see him first and see how he reacts. If he has nothing to hide, he won't need to worry and shouldn't give me any grief. Yes—I'll see Victor first.'

'You'd best take me with you. I don't think it's safe questioning suspects on your own if they are possible murderers,' said Martha, frowning her disapproval.'

'If you insist, but I've been doing this for years—remember? I'll call him now and see if he can make time for us to visit today.'

'I believe he lives on his own. I've driven past his little place just outside the village, but I've never been inside his home. It always looks dark, as he keeps his curtains drawn, which matches his miserable demeanour.'

♫ ♫ ♫

Ann trotted up to the old oak door of the house with Martha scurrying behind her. She hesitated before knocking on the door.

'Are you sure this is it? I had visions of a shabby little villa.'

'I know, but I've rarely seen a window open, and the curtains are always closed like this,' she said, pointing at the dated wooden windows.

'Come on—let's do it,' said Ann, lurching forward and knocking firmly on the door. There was a rummaging sound from inside, and then a head popped furtively from behind the curtain. In an instant, Victor flung the door open.

'So, what is it you want, did you say? Oh ... you've come too,' he said, glaring at Ann and casting a glance with a sneer towards Martha.

This time Ann flashed her police identity card in front of him. 'Alright if we come in?' Ann asserted bravely.

'I'm glad I had a major clean up this morning—otherwise, you wouldn't find anywhere to sit. I don't know what you want with me—your lot have been all over this property looking for a euphonium they think I've flogged and all they found was my own instrument, not the one they wanted. An insult that is!'

The two women glanced around the room to see piles of old newspapers stacked high in the corner and along the wall.

After they sat down, Ann felt the need to open a window, almost gagging on the musty smell in the room.

'I get a bit of asthma—mind if I have a window open?' said Martha, holding her hand to her throat. She wanted to add that the dust in the room was giving her an attack.

'Humph!' Victor grunted, as he traipsed over to the window and pushed it open.

Ann went into detail as simply as she could, justifying the need to check spanners belonging to band members with the Marco branding. Victor tensed, clenching his fists, his neck flushing.

'Is that why you're here? Well, I'm sorry to waste your time, but I don't have tools like that. In fact, it's a long while since I've done any handyman work since I left the farm.'

Martha and Ann shared a wary glance.

'Are you sure, Victor? They come in a set of five.'

'I don't need those things now. I used to have all that clobber on the farm but left it all behind when we sold up. That was before it all came tumbling down around me,' he said, frozen tears forming in his eyes.'

'I'm sorry to hear you've had to leave your farm, Victor. It must have been quite a wrench if you excuse the pun.'

'Forgive me for not offering you ladies tea or coffee—I'm clean out of milk unless you can take it black.'

'Not for me thanks, Victor,' said Martha.

'Don't worry about us,' said Ann, now eager to drag more information from him.

'I need to let you know that as part of our murder enquiry, we are interviewing family members of Riverlea Brassholes. Therefore, I will pay a visit to your family in Cambridge.'

'What family is this—the ex-wife, you mean?'

'Yes, Grace is her name, isn't it?'

'I don't know how raking up all that misery will help. You police lot have a strange way of going about things.'

He bent over to pat his ginger cat on the head and then pulled it onto his lap. 'These creatures give fewer hassles than two-legged ones.'

'I guess you miss Grace. Would you like to get back together again, if you don't mind me asking?'

'Well, that is another strange question to ask, but seeing you are so inquisitive—yes, I would like everything to be how it used to be when we were happily working together running the farm, but I'm afraid that horse has bolted.'

'Look—we won't keep you any longer. We may have to question you some more, but for now, that will do.'

As Victor accompanied the women to the Land Rover, Ann glanced toward his garage.

'If you don't mind—can you show me what vehicles you have? That is a routine part of our enquiry too,' she said, starting to head over there.

'Ah, if you insist,' he sniped.

To the women's surprise, when he opened the garage, in one corner stood an old Harley Davidson motorbike parked next to a Toyota Corolla hatchback.

'So, you're a motorbike enthusiast. I like a Harley—mind if you start it for me? It's a long while since I've seen any—I rode one during my youth.' She bent over to inspect the trophy. 'What's that on your muffler—a silencer?'

Oh, yeah—Grace insisted I got one when we were dealing with all the stress of having to give up our cows due to low milk prices. The noise got on her nerves,' he said, starting up the engine.

'Goodness—the engine is certainly quiet,' said Martha.

'We'd best get off now—thanks, Victor. I'll be in touch if we need you for further questioning. Oh, would you mind giving me Grace's address? The station can look it up, but it will be quicker this way.'

Victor obliged, jotting it down on a scrap of paper Ann handed him.

'If you visit Grace ... um ... give her my regards ... tell her I miss her and Jill.'

Chapter Thirty

'Guilt is written all over his face, don't you think?' said Martha, nodding her head as Ann drove them home. 'He even denied having any other spanners. He won't admit to owning a set if he knows we're trying to match them.'

'Don't worry—if the police and I believe he is a person of interest, we can get a warrant and search his house, unless he has removed them from his property.'

'What did you think of the motorbike with a silencer on the muffler? Didn't you think that was suspect?'

'I know what you mean. Very handy to zip in and out of a car park without drawing attention to oneself. But we have no proof of anything like this—no evidence and you haven't got a case.'

Martha drooped as if Ann's last statement put the final nail in the coffin, and their attempts of finding the killer were futile.

'Let's go for a day trip to leafy old Cambridge. I'm very partial to that tiny village and beautiful Lake Karapiro.'

'Fabulous idea. There's a quaint café by the church where we could have lunch and some cute antique shops.'

'I'll take poor Scout along for the ride—he loves going on trips, and I haven't taken him for a while.'

When they arrived home, Scout whimpered on the back doorstep wanting to go inside. Ann opened the door, and instead of following her inside, the dog beckoned her to come outside with him. Martha looked around to see what the commotion was.

'He's upset about something. I hope it's not that awful person out there who threw the doped beefsteak into the yard.'

Martha dashed on ahead with Ann in tow and to her disgust Scout led her to an all-time, horticultural disaster.

'Oh, no! Heaven forbid—she's been at it again. Just when I thought she had grown out of these antics.'

Ann restrained the belly laugh that threatened to erupt from her as she watched the pink pig routing around on the wrong side of Martha's picket fence. She had demolished an entire bed of ripe strawberries that would have kept Martha in jam for a year.

It appeared Hyacinth had found a hole under the fence and routed away at it until it was large enough for the rotund body to crawl under. She stood looking at the women with her face covered in red strawberry juice, the sight of which caused them both to crack up with laughter.

'I suppose this goes with the territory when one has a pig as a pet,' said Ann. 'Just give me the word, and I'll get you a retired police dog.'

'I couldn't part with this one, though. I've got used to her. It's my fault for not checking my garden to make sure she can't get in there. Anyway—let's sit at the table on the veranda before it gets dark and talk about our next plan of action. We make an exceptional team we do,' said Martha, leaving Hyacinth to finish her dastardly work in the garden before she banished her to the orchard.

'She may as well complete what she began, as there's nothing left of my crop. I'll plant something else there now, and she can clean up before I do that.'

Ann raised her eyebrows. *Who would have a pig for a pet?'* she thought, as she fastened Scout's lead and took him on his long-awaited walk to the park.

♫ ♫ ♫

'That was a straight run down the freeway, wasn't it? Whenever I've come down here, the road is usually busy,' said Martha, winding down her window to search for a café for lunch.

'How long ago was that? I've always found the road from Auckland to Hamilton busy.'

'Oh, I suppose it would be ten years ago since I've been down this way. Last time was with Frank on his birthday. We came down for a car show.'

Ann pulled up outside a nostalgic, wooden church.

'What are we stopping here for?' Martha craned her neck to see where she was taking her.

'Around the back is a lovely café that makes home-cooked food—you'll see.'

'Seeing that we stopped on the way down to let Scout do his thing on the side of the road, I'll leave him in the car with the windows half-open,' said Ann, pouring what was left of her water bottle into a dog bowl and placing it on the floor of the vehicle.

'Let's go,' she said, leading the way with Martha in tow.

After they ate lunch, Ann waltzed up to the counter to ask the shop assistant how to get to Grace's house.

On the way back to the car, She hesitated. 'Would you like to potter around the antique shops for a while? I don't mind going to see Grace on my own.'

'I'd love to pop into one or two of them before we visit her. Have we got time?'

'Tell you what—how about you do that, and I'd like to take a drive to an old haunt out by Lake Karapiro where I used to do a lot of kayaking in my student years. I'll meet you back here by the church in an hour.'

'Great, I'll be ready. See you then.'

Ann took off to find the camping site by the river she frequented during her university days.

'Here we are, Scout. Now you can go for a run,' she said, clipping the dog's elasticized lead to his collar and letting him ramble on the grassy river bank.

After the dog had finished sniffing around the riverbank, Ann sat down on a patch of ground staring into the ripples of the water.

Where to now if nothing develops from this visit with Grace and her daughter?

She slumped forward, resting her face on her arms as she leaned on her knees, her eyes fixated on a kingfisher which appeared on a tree stump in the water.

Maybe you've lost the touch, and it's time to give up the game.

♫ ♫ ♫

One thing Ann enjoyed about being a private investigator was the morning and afternoon teas offered her by clients, especially the freshly baked scones and cakes.

Grace and her daughter, Jill also lavished their visitors with an elaborate welcome, as they were the first band members they had seen in years, or at least since Victor had walked out. Together with him they too had been avid supporters of the Haversham Hooters.

After they broke the ice, Grace opened up to Martha and Ann telling how hard life was for her and Victor before they lost their farm in Haversham, South Auckland.

'Milk prices plummeted, and we couldn't keep hold of our stock. The bank eventually foreclosed our mortgage, and to avoid bankruptcy, it forced us to sell at a loss. Farming had been our life. We raised our children on the farm and the little band, the Haversham Hooters was the only thing that gave Victor any purpose in life when everything else was going down the drainpipe.'

'Of course,' Martha blurted—I forgot that was Victor's previous band. He says nothing about it.'

'No, he won't. He would find it difficult to talk about, as he didn't want to leave. He had to move to Auckland for work, and there he purchased a tiny cottage in Cotesville.'

'You know why we're here, don't you?'

'Yes, you mentioned you were investigating the death of a bandsman. Do you think it's suspicious?'

Until this point, Grace's daughter, Jill, had said nothing, but suddenly she found her tongue.

'You mean he has been murdered?'

'We don't know that for sure,' said Ann, 'There is evidence he had been assaulted. The killer made it look as though a tuba had fallen off a shelf and injured him, but the wounds revealed otherwise.'

'Wow, a murder in a band room!' Jill spouted. 'Then why are you questioning us?' she asked.

'We need to match two tools we found near the band room that could be evidence. If your father owned the same tools, confirmation of this could clear his name.'

'What—Dad, a suspect? Mum, what are they saying?' she retorted, glaring at her mother.

'Well, Victor may be a lot of things, but he would never kill anyone. You must be mistaken thinking he was capable of murder,' said Grace, with a pinched face.

Ann placed the spanners in front of Grace. 'Pick one up and tell me if you recognise them. Did Victor own any of these?'

'What did Victor say about them?'

'He said he couldn't remember having any but may have left them behind when he left the farm.'

Ann felt guilty lying about that but wanted to catch Victor out if she could get the truth from his ex-wife.

'Let me inspect them,' said Grace, squinting and looking around for her glasses. 'Ah, here they are.'

She picked up each tool looking closely at the imprint and then sat quietly for a few minutes.

'He had a set of these—I bought him one online for his birthday about two years before we sold the farm. They were expensive, and he took good care of them. When he left walked out, he told me to give his tools to my son as he wouldn't need them any longer.'

'Where is your son, if you don't mind me asking, in case I need to verify this?'

'He lives down South in Queenstown. I'm sure he would oblige.'

'Thanks—I'll get those details off you before we leave.'

Grace continued to give the two women Victor's hard-luck story.

'Victor's maternal grandmother donated the Sylvester Cup to the band after his grandfather died. That man had been the founder and stalwart of Haversham Hooters, which was an anchor for all the local farmers. They struggled with depression after suffering significant losses due to droughts and setbacks in the dairy industry. Music was Victor's life, as it had been his father's and often the only thing that gave him the motivation to live. Winning the Sylvester Cup each year was the one thing that gave them all self-esteem and a sense of purpose. Some of our band members wanted to turn what was traditionally a rural social band into an A-grade contesting one. Our committee had voted fiercely against it when Victor and his father were players, and until this day have kept them out.'

Grace saw both women out to their vehicle, and before Ann stepped into the driver's seat, the woman took her arm gently and said, 'Tell him I miss him too—we both miss him, and it's time to come home.'

When Ann and Martha left Grace and her daughter, they were sure they had found a motive for all the nasty attacks at the band. But would Victor be also capable of murder? Grace convinced her that although he had become abusive towards the end of their marriage because of the pressure he was under, she didn't think he had it in him to murder a fellow bandsman. But as Ann had already said to Martha, from all her years dealing with criminals, wolves often come in harmless-looking clothing.

'Well, that was an eye-opener,' said Ann, as they walked towards her vehicle. I don't think it implicates Grace or Jill in any way. That excludes them, but I'm not sure about Victor. You hop into the car—I've got to make a quick call to Isaac.'

While Martha stepped into the vehicle, Ann took out her cell phone to make the call.

'Hi Isaac—well, that is a turn-up for the books, for sure. This will put a whole new slant on things. Yes, I'll be there—I'll be right over the minute I get back.'

Before Ann started the engine, Martha, who was sitting listening to her wide-eyed, was eager for information.

'Isaac said the police have had a woman come forward as a result of their invitation for information from the public about the night in question—the Saturday evening Chad was attacked.'

'What happened, and who was she?'

'I don't know—he couldn't elaborate over the phone, but I'm soon going to find out.'

Driving back to Auckland, Ann kept thinking that they could be barking up the wrong tree where Victor was concerned. This case would take a lot longer to solve than she initially thought and right now, she felt as though she was not on top of her game. She needed a breakthrough.

As her Land Rover pulled into Martha's driveway after a long drive home on the busy motorway, Ann wanted nothing more than to get inside the house and soak in a hot bath, letting the cares of the day wash over her. But this wasn't going to happen right now. She had a murder to solve, and while she was on a case, she could not let her guard down, no matter how tired she was.

'You hop out and take Scout inside with you while I slip over to see Isaac. I won't be long hopefully.'

'Sure thing—and I'll feed him too. I'll have a meal ready by the time you get back. Unless you want to call into the takeaway up the road and get us a Chow Mein or something.'

'I'll do that—you'll be weary like me. We'll keep it simple tonight.'

Chapter Thirty-one

Isaac sat drumming his fingers on his wooden desk, waiting while Ann read through the report.

'Well, this is a surprise—hopefully, the breakthrough we are waiting for.'

The woman who had responded to the police soliciting help from the public had seen unusual behaviour from someone on the night in question—the Saturday Chad had been attacked. She drove from her home in Riverlea to collect her son from soccer at the sports field opposite the band room. As she slowed near the entrance, a white long-wheelbase Ute almost side-swiped her vehicle. The young male driver had bolted out of the band room car park veering over the wrong side, forcing her off the road. It happened so fast she had no time to note the vehicle's details, but she knew she had seen it around the village occasionally. After he had disappeared, she glanced in the direction of the band room car park and under the moonlight noticed there was a shiny, blue Ford parked next to a clump of trees which she thought strange, as there were no lights on in the hall. By the time she had picked up her son, she'd forgotten all about it and didn't pursue it further until she heard the police asking the public for help.

'I suppose we're going to have to track down every white Ute with a long-wheelbase in the area and beyond. There can't be that many of them.'

'You're right,' said Isaac. I've already got officers on the trail as you speak. You said you checked out Victor Saltman's vehicles, didn't you?'

'Yep, he only has a Toyota Corolla saloon car and an old Harley Davidson bike.'

'Perhaps we've been on a merry chase regarding Victor. Ah, just a moment.'

Another officer hauled him away into the corridor. He returned to his office, beaming.

'That was Queenstown. After you rang me about Victor's son and the spanner set, I sent an officer around to his house to follow that up as he lives nearby the station. Sure enough, he showed them a full set of Marco spanners, bar a small one the size that was found jammed in that copier machine. He said he'd never had one—those were the only wrenches his father gave him. So, it doesn't let Victor completely off the hook, I'm afraid. He could still have sabotaged the printer and perhaps committed the rest of the vandalism. But we need to focus on the murder enquiry for now.'

'And what about the missing euphonium? Those things are worth a packet and would be like bees to a honey pot for a burglar,' said Ann.

Isaac hesitated. 'So now you're insinuating that it could have been a burglary gone belly up.'

'It is beginning to look that way. Did the woman get the number of that Ute?'

'She tried but said it was too dark. She did recognise the face, though. Some young, scruffy character she has seen driving through the village now and then with unkempt long hair.'

'Surely he is known to you lot. It's a small place for him to go unnoticed and he probably has a record.'

'The woman is going to look at an identity kit tomorrow, and we'll go from there.'

♫ ♫ ♫

Three Days Later

Ann longed to take the day off as she sat eating breakfast with Martha on the veranda the next morning. She sat with her dossier going through the list of band members and had run out of people with a possible motive to harm Chad and carry out the rest of the malicious attacks. She had excluded the members who had been away the day Will had received the chemical burns and the rest of the band members she had already eliminated from her enquiry. That still left Victor with more than ever, a motive for bringing the band down. According to his ex-wife, he had been obsessed with banding to the exclusion of the rest of his family. She'd called it a psychotic obsession.

As for the young man in the white LWB Ute, he was probably doing something in the car park entirely unrelated, like smoking dope or looking for a car to break into, which he probably had done, as a window of Chad's vehicle had been smashed.

Ann felt sick at the thought of Victor being sent to prison and breaking the news to his wife, who believed he would return home. That was the part of her previous job as Detective Inspector, which was the most difficult—telling a family member that their loved one was going to jail.

'Ann—your cell phone's ringing,' called Martha, scurrying out onto the veranda.

Ann nodded and smiled, taking the phone from her.

'Hi Isaac, what have you got for me? Good news, I hope.'

'We tracked down a white LWB Ute parked outside a dairy about ten kilometres out-of-town fitting the witness's description. She had identified the owner in a lineup, and although it was night time, the entrance to the band room was well-lit by the moon, and she was clear it was him.'

'Excellent! Have you brought him in for questioning?'

'Yes, he's now in custody, but I need you here to correlate the information you have on the spate of misdeeds in the band room.'

'What about Martha—should I bring her?'

'No, not at this stage—it is purely a police matter. She may have to give evidence in court at a later date.'

'I'll be on my way. See you soon.'

When Ann turned around, it was apparent Martha had been standing listening to the whole conversation.

'Don't take it personally, Martha. They don't usually have lay people sitting in on police interviews.'

'I'm not offended at all. I follow enough police dramas to know that's the drill,' she said chuckling.

'Off you go—I can't wait to hear all the news, and I'm hoping it will put Victor in the clear. I'm beginning to feel sorry for him now after that sad story his wife told us.'

'I know what you mean—I concur.'

♫ ♫ ♫

It had been several years since Ann interviewed a person in custody, especially a murder case. Of course, she knew that Isaac would question Johnny, but he would expect Ann to do her part too.

208

When Ann perused the report that Isaac placed in front of her on his office desk, she stopped aghast. The alleged offender on the form shared the same address as Tom, who owned the orchard next to the band room. Before entering the interview room, she pointed it out to Isaac, going into details about her and Martha's visit to the old farmer.

With her daybook and dossier tucked under her arm, she followed Isaac into the room. The accused sat at the desk with his head in his hands while Ann looked with disgust at his long, unkempt hair that appeared unwashed in months.

They informed the man in his early twenties that a witness saw him in the band car park where a vehicle window had been smashed, and a man had been found dead inside the hall. Isaac first asked Ann to read him his rights when being questioned, which she knew off pat after years of repetition.

Isaac did the interviewing and allowed Ann to assist. During the session, he cautioned the offender that he was recording the interview.

While he denied breaking into Chad's vehicle, the suspect hedged around the discussion about his reason for being in the car park, saying that he was just doing some joyriding.

'Now listen carefully, Johnny,' said Isaac curtly. 'While Detective Grieves and I interview you, police officers are in the process of searching your home with a warrant. If there's anything you want to tell us about—something they might find that could incriminate you, it's best to let us know now. It could lessen your sentence if you are later charged.'

There was a rap at the door. A police constable entered and asked Isaac to come to the door where he handed him a document while they whispered to each other.

Isaac thanked him and returned to the interviewing table where the four sat.

'Officers have found many stolen goods in the way of car parts on your property, but the object of most importance to us is the euphonium they discovered. They have checked the serial number, and it appears to be the instrument that went missing from the Riverlea Brassholes band instrument room the night of the murder of Chad Bates.'

The colour swiftly drained from Johnny's thin face, as he suddenly aged by ten years. He demanded a solicitor.

As he couldn't afford a defence lawyer, the police contacted a legal aid attorney who arrived in a short time and hauled him out into another room to talk with him privately while Isaac stalled the interview. When Johnny re-entered the room with the woman who had introduced herself as Ruth, she cautioned him not to answer questions unless she gave him the nod of approval.

There was a rap at the door. Isaac attended to the constable standing behind the door who whispered a message and handed him a report before Isaac shut the door and sat back at the table.

'I'm restarting the recording.'

Johnny clenched his fists and began grinding his teeth. Isaac handed Ruth the document which she perused and thrust back at him. He passed it to Ann.

'Mmm, it seems you've been a busy man in this neighbourhood. You have quite a racket, haven't you—dealing in stolen goods I see?'

'No comment,' he said, watching Ruth's face.

'We can corroborate this, but what particularly interests me is the euphonium you have taken from the Riverlea Brassholes' band room. We have the serial number, so there's no getting away from that. They have also found a small quantity of a drug called *Acepro*—a controlled substance that you should not have in your possession. Any explanation?'

Johnny's face began to twitch. Ruth requested time with her client alone while both detectives left the room and waited outside the door.

'Well—this puts a whole new slant on everything. We need to get a confession from him,' said Isaac, frowning.

'But what I don't understand is why he is living in Tom's orchard on the other side of the five-acre block.'

'It appears Johnny is his grandson.'

'Oh, no!' Ann blurted. 'Poor Tom. Why would Johnny need to go to those lengths? From what I gather from Martha, Tom is fairly well off.'

'You and I can visit Tom after this. There is a lot more to this than a straight burglary.'

Ruth called them back into the room while Isaac switched the recorder back on.

'Well, do you have an explanation for having the instrument in your house? Did you carry out the vandalism of the vehicle in the carpark?'

Johnny darted a glance at his lawyer who gave him a nod.

'I desperately needed the money and hoped to find a car stereo or something I could sell. I went into my car boot for my leather gloves and a crowbar and then smashed the front passenger window with a rag over it. I was gutted, as there was nothing but an old car radio.'

'What did you do after you broke the window?' asked Ann.

'I threw the crowbar back into my boot and was about to drive off when I remembered there were valuable instruments in that building. I took my overalls from the boot. Those are the ones I use when spraying, and they entirely cover my clothing. After pulling them on, I took out a pair of old trainers. I always buy them cheap for doing burglaries and burn them afterwards.

'You always come prepared?' asked Ann.

'Yep—ready for any opportunity, like this one.'

'I suppose, like all professional crooks, you wore gloves too?'

'For sure,' he replied glibly.

'I've always wanted to get my hands on one of those instruments,' Johnny replied.

Ruth looked at him and nodded again.

'I quickly got out and stuck my head through the door. It was quiet, and the hall appeared empty, but there was a faint light towards the back of the hall.'

'Did you have a weapon in your hand when you entered the building?' asked Isaac.

Johnny muttered something that neither of the detectives could hear.

'Speak up, so everyone can hear you,' said Ruth.

He hesitated to look back at Ruth and stammered, 'No, I did not. I just intended to grab an instrument and run, so I crept along the side of the hall and peeked into the dimly lit room where there were a lot of large instruments ... you know ... those big tuba things and some others like that but smaller, perched on a shelf.'

'Did anyone see you—who was there?'

'I couldn't see anyone at first, and then I noticed a faint glow coming from the other side of the hall and heard someone rummaging around inside a large cupboard.'

Ann glanced at Isaac. 'That will have been the storeroom on the opposite side of the hall. The night light is feeble there.'

'What did you plan to do when you walked into the hall?' asked Isaac.

'I was just looking for something I could sell that was worth my while ... until ... then it happened.'

He put his face in his hands as his voice petered off into a quaver as he shook his head. 'He shouldn't have lurched at me—otherwise, I wouldn't have done it. He frightened me.

'What did you do, Johnny?' urged Isaac.

'Stop—you don't have to answer this until we are in court under oath,' said Ruth, sharply.

'Yes, I do ... I want to! I'm not a cold-blooded murderer. I didn't intend for anyone to get hurt.'

Isaac flashed a glance of relief at Ann, raising his eyebrows. He pressed again.

'Continue telling us what happened when you went to the instrument room?'

'I need a cigarette ... please?'

'You can't smoke in here. After you've answered our questions, an officer can take you out the back for a smoke.'

Johnny began twisting his fingers, almost dislocating his knuckles.

'I grabbed hold of the euphonium—the one the cops found in my house and was about to run to my car. A tall streak of a fellow came rushed at me from across the hall yelling he would call the police. He lurched at me, and I ducked and then panicked as I saw him reach for his phone from a jacket lying on the ground. As he bent over, I picked up a wrench from his toolkit that lay open and bashed him on the head. He crashed to the ground like a felled kauri tree.'

'Did you stop to see if he was alive?' asked Ann.

'Are you joking? I didn't think I'd smacked him that hard—I was out of there. I didn't know I'd killed him,' he snivelled.

'So, you didn't lay a tuba over him as a cover to make it look as though it had fallen on him?' asked Isaac, determined to get a full confession.

'No, I didn't. The tuba went flying as he hit the ground and fell on top of him.'

'When the victim lurched at you, did he have anything in his hand which he could use as a weapon to assault you?'

Johnny grimaced, shaking his head. 'No, but he came up behind me so quietly he took me by surprise and sprang at me. If only he'd let me run off with the instrument, he'd still be alive. I didn't intend to kill him—I was frightened and over-reacted.'

'What were you wearing when you entered the band hall that night?' Asked Ann, clearing her throat.

'What did you do with the overalls and shoes you wore after you assaulted the victim?'

'I burnt them at the back of the orchard.'

'Yes, police officers discovered the remains of a fire recently, and we have had it tested,' said Isaac.

Ann read through the forensic results which stated that although there had been a bonfire at the orchard, the investigators had found nothing they could use as evidence. She continued to peruse her notes and then handed him a document.

'We have a long list of malicious deeds that occurred in the band room during the last few months. I want you to look at this list and tell us if there are any that you have committed.'

He looked through the file raising his eyebrows and shaking his head, handing it back to her.

'Only one—the drugged meat for the dog.'

'What on earth would you want to do that for?' said Ann, trying not to let on the dog belonged to her.

'I knew that there was an old Indian motorbike in the woman's shed by the fence which her husband had kept as an heirloom. I wanted to get at it, but that darn dog appeared on the property recently. I got hold of a sedative from a dealer and used it to knock him out. I never intended to kill him, and I see he's still alive and kicking.'

'Why were you so desperate for money? I heard you'd been working for your grandfather in the orchard before he retired. Haven't you had any work since? And you live on his property—surely, he wouldn't charge you much rent,' said Isaac.

'He doesn't charge me rent as long as I mow the rows between the trees in the orchard—I use a ride-on. I also have to weed the property.'

'You haven't answered my question. Are you working right now?'

'Yep—granddad sorted a job for me in the avocado packing shed down the road until I decide what I want to do with my degree.'

'What degree? We know that you were living in Wellington and attending university there. Did you graduate?'

'I didn't finish but almost. I've still got three papers to do—horticultural management. Granddad paid for it all. When I get my degree, he promised I could start up the orchard again with modern equipment, and project manage the building of a new packing shed.'

'That's a pity you didn't finish. So how did you get into debt that bad that you had to resort to crime?' Ann asked.

'I started smoking a lot of cannabis in Wellington and partying heaps. I ran up huge debts and used a loan shark to pay it off. I've only drip-fed him with what I could afford, as I'm finishing my degree by distant study and picking up what work I can, which doesn't pay for much. He has been sending me threatening text messages and malicious phone calls saying he will harm my mother if I don't pay the full amount now. I haven't been able to sleep at night, and I owe him thousands.'

'Have you kept those messages? I can charge him,' said Isaac.

'Yes, I have. I use another phone now, and he doesn't have my number nor my address.'

'Right—give me the details, and I'll get onto that. Are sure you didn't commit any of the other malicious acts?' asked Ann with an empathetic tone.

Johnny's face turned red, and he stood up. 'Look—you're going to put me away for murder, so what does this matter? All those stupid things you have on the list have no relevance to my conviction. I'm not answering any more questions.'

Ann wasn't finished with him yet.

'Sit down,' Ruth whispered to Johnny.

'I don't understand why you didn't ask your grandfather for help. I know he would have been able to bail you out and all this could have been prevented.'

'Because he has done enough for me. I didn't want to let him down, as he had high hopes for me. I was so ashamed.'

'And how did you obtain the drug, *Acepro*? I suppose you were one of the idiots who broke into the vet clinic last year.'

'No! That wasn't me. I bought it on the black market.'

'Perhaps you can help us with the names of these racketeers as well as your loan shark. It could have a favourable impact on you getting a lighter sentence,' warned Isaac.

'That's enough—you've got your confession, and I'll take it from here,' Ruth snapped. 'We could be looking at self-defence with this case, so don't get carried away,' she said bluntly. 'The victim was over six-foot-tall and muscle-bound compared to my client's smaller stature. I'll stop you on this note, thanks.'

Ruth spoke to them alone while her client was still in the interview room.

'I'm just letting you know that there are issues relating to the lad's mental health and I will raise this in court with a psychiatric report.'

After Ruth left and Johnny was taken to a holding cell, Ann and Isaac were stunned at what had just unfolded before them—especially Ann, after finding out that this was Tom's grandson.

Ann nudged Isaac. 'Come on—I'm bursting to interview poor Tom regarding all this. I feel sorry for the man, but I know I can't let it influence me in any way. I couldn't see Johnny as a killer, not at all. He looks like a lost soul, though. I suppose the best we can get him is involuntary manslaughter.'

Chapter Thirty-two

Ann had already warned Tom she would bring Isaac with her on this visit. He'd asked over the phone whether Martha would come and had sounded somewhat disappointed that she wasn't able to.

When they arrived, Isaac let Ann soften the blow by telling Tom the grim news about Johnny—that the police had arrested him on remand without bail. He collapsed back into his seat.

'I'm sorry, Tom. But there's so much about Johnny that we need to hear—especially about his background.'

Tom cooperated going to considerable lengths telling the detectives about the mitigating circumstances of Johnny's tragic past and how he had helped him get his life on track.

Ann recorded the details in her black book.

Johnny's father died of terminal cancer when the boy, an only child was fifteen. His mother, Tom's daughter, Harriet, couldn't cope with him when he went off the rails as a teen, and after going to university, he got into more strife there. He accumulated debt through riotous living and dropped out of his course.

Finally, at her wit's end and on the verge of a breakdown, Harriet begged her parents to take him in. Tom trained him up for work in the orchard, and he flourished there, eventually living in a workers cottage on the far side of the property and managing staff. He told how his influences changed Johnny, who began to clean up his act.

Recently he received threats from a loan shark, unbeknown to Tom and started doing petty crime to pay him off. Johnny was too ashamed to ask for help as he'd already had a lot of handouts from him—he was determined he'd find the money his own way.

Ann looked up from her notebook. 'Did you know he had got into crime recently?'

'No, but I guessed he must be in trouble of some sort. I looked inside his house one day, and it was as though a tornado had ripped through it. He was living rough, and I could see he wasn't eating. He never told me about the assault on Chad, but he said he had done some things he was ashamed of and was trying to sort his life out.'

'When was this?' Asked Isaac.

'Only a week ago. He told me that a loan shark had threatened him. I said I would clear the debt and get the mongrel off his back. Unfortunately, that horse had already bolted—it was too late.'

His eyes clouded over, and his voice croaked. 'What will happen to him now—will he go to prison?'

'We hope not, but we need to convey this information to Ruth, his lawyer. It could help prove there were extenuating circumstances and hopefully we can get him a reduced sentence, or even better a non-custodial term.'

'He can serve that here—I'll take care of him,' said Tom, sniffing loudly.

'We'll keep you posted, but first I'll arrange for a family visitor pass for you. You both need to talk.'

'Thanks, Isaac. I don't know how to tell my daughter—this will break her heart.'

'Maybe you could hold off from telling her until the hearing. You could distress her unnecessarily.'

'What are his chances of staying out of prison?' he asked.

'Good so long as Ruth plays the game, which I'm sure she will. She's a talented lawyer and has a heart for the underdog.'

'Johnny was acting under duress after being bullied by a loan shark. He had no intentions of killing Chad that day and freaked out when Chad went to call the police. He was just running scared, and even though he struck him on the head, it wasn't with intent to kill, but to fend him off.'

'Oh, Ann, I hope you're right,' said Tom, holding back the tears.'

'She's right,' said Isaac. 'He has a lot going for him, and if you say you'll stand by and support him through his university studies so he can run your orchard, I'm sure we'll win.'

Ann nudged Isaac pointing at her wristwatch.

'We've got to get on our way, sorry. We can show ourselves out.'

Tom appeared sad to see them leave, alone in his sadness.

'Let's get the ball rolling and get that family visitor's pass for him,' said Ann, picking up her daybook and trotting out the door.

♫ ♫ ♫

'What a day that was. You won't believe the shenanigans that have been going on in quiet Riverlea,' said Ann, as Martha passed her a late-night hot toddy.

'It was one of the busiest days I've had. I'm sorry I wasn't able to get to your band practice this week—I'm afraid I'll have to forgo playing with you all any further, as seeing these cases out to the end is all I have time for right now. It was only ever going to be temporary—my playing in your band.'

Martha passed her an Anzac biscuit. 'I understand—I knew we only had you on-loan while you bailed us out. If it weren't for you, we wouldn't be holding this cup,' she said, pointing to the glossy, brass trophy on the mantelpiece.

'I'm concerned about Tom. I have arranged for him to visit Johnny in the morning. Would you like to drop by his house afterwards and offer a bit of support? I think he'll need it and you're the best person for it.'

'Oh, dear—that doesn't sound good. How long will it be before Johnny gets a court hearing?'

'We are trying to push it along, so hopefully, it will be before the end of the week.'

'I'll pop round to see Tom tomorrow afternoon. It must worry him sick.'

'Thanks, Martha. I'm bushed and going off to bed. Big day tomorrow, and we still have to see if Johnny is connected with the malicious incidents. I hope not, as it won't help his case. I'll see you in the morning.'

Chapter Thirty-three

Guess who crawled out of the woodwork

A week later, while Ann walked Scout down by the river hoping and praying that Johnny's lawyer would get him a lenient sentence, Isaac called her.

'You'd better get down to the station as soon as you can. I've got Victor sitting in the interview room with an officer, ready to confess.'

'Goodness!' Ann blurted. 'He has finally come to his senses. I wonder what prompted his to do this—I'll be right there as soon as I walk my dog back to the house. Give me twenty minutes.'

'I'll try and keep him sweet until then but come as soon as you can. I don't want him to change his mind and shoot through on me.'

'Will do—see you soon.'

Ann had mixed feelings about Victor wanting to confess. She'd hoped he wasn't the culprit of the malicious deeds in the band room as the words of his ex-wife, Grace and the image of his sad daughter lingered uppermost in her mind. *Tell Victor it's time for him to come home*—that's what Grace had said to her. The recollection of this brought tears to this almost hardened detective's eyes. It had melted not only her heart but also Victor's after she had conveyed that message to him earlier in the week.

♫ ♫ ♫

'He has his own solicitor in there,' said Isaac, pointing to the interview room. 'He's getting pretty agitated and looks in a right state. I think he might respond best to a female interrogating him rather than me. Would you mind conducting the interview, Ann?'

Ann was stunned being caught on the hop and unprepared for the task. Hesitating, she recalled the look on Grace's face when she had asked her to tell Victor it was time to come home.

When she entered the room with Isaac, Ann was taken aback at how dishevelled Victor appeared since she last saw him. He was unshaven, and his face was gaunt. She felt like taking a comb to his hair.

Ann's line of questioning didn't take long before Victor spewed out,' I did it all—the nasty pranks in the band room—it was me. But I didn't kill Chad—I didn't touch him!'

A weight suddenly lifted from Ann's shoulders as her tight neck muscles loosened.

'We suspected it might be you—but why? What motive could a bandsman have to inflict such pain and duress on his fellow bandsmen?'

Victor hung his head, his eyes refusing to meet Ann's. She waited while he sat wringing his hands. His lawyer said nothing and held back too.

He finally raised his head and blurted, 'Plain selfishness and an obsession with ambition!'

'I don't understand, Victor,' Ann replied, shooting a glance at Isaac raising her eyebrows.

'You have to know about my background with banding—how Haversham Hooters was once a humble country brass band that was founded by my grandfather, Basil Sylvester. He spent hours tutoring young players to become accomplished brass band members and my father carried it on. It was all we had as a struggling farming community, and when the wool prices plummeted, some farmers were suicidal. The only thing that kept us going was our local brass band. We looked forward to it each week, and it gave us such a lift. But it was all men, and the women were stuck on the farms with nothing to lift their spirits. Just like my grandfather, my father was obsessed with it. It was his whole life and nothing else mattered. He ate, drank and breathed it to the exclusion of all else.'

Ann interjected. 'How did your mother put up with it—did she object?'

'Granddad Sylvester was her father, and she was used to him ruling the roost with the band. It had been a way of life. When he died, she donated the brass trophy called the Sylvester Cup to the Provincial Band Organisation as a contest prize. It is an annual event.'

'What has all this got to do with your motive for harming band members?' Isaac asked.

Victor scowled at him. 'I'm getting to that part!' he snapped, looking sideways at his lawyer who nodded her approval to carry on.

'I became like my father, and as farming became tougher and it seemed impossible to keep up with increasing costs, I tried to bury the pain of it all by throwing myself into music even more. I was president of the band and insisted we practice twice a week. I forgot about Grace and the children and became self-centred, I guess.'

Victor's lawyer leant over and asked softly, 'Where are you heading with all this?'

'I'm trying to make everyone understand how my obsession with the brass band to the exclusion of all others caused the neglect and breakdown of my family life. Although the economy destroyed our ability to hold on to the farm, my selfishness was the reason I lost my family. My son took off down south, and I neglected my wife. We had to sell the farm to avoid bankruptcy, and there was no work again Haversham. After we separated, I reluctantly took a job in Rodney County as a stockbroker and bought a cottage in Cotesville.'

Ann wondered if he was ever going to get to the point. It was as if he was trying to formulate a story to make them all see him as a victim—but was he? Ann wondered.

'We had always held the cup—Haversham Hooters, I mean, and last year to my horror, Riverlea Brassholes took it off us by a few points. What angered me was that my band colleagues in Haversham had all been hardworking farmers struggling to stay alive, more or less and didn't come from A grade bands or such like. We never took part in the National Band Championships and were only a social band. It was a place where we, as farmers could go to chill and unwind, and we wanted no part in graded contest bands.'

'Tell us why you were so destructive, Victor,' said Isaac, to Victor's annoyance. Ann hoped her colleague would let her lead the questioning as she could see by the way the accused glared at Isaac that he was irritated by him, just at a crucial point in his confession.

'I couldn't stand seeing those Riverlea Brassholes swanning in and out of the practices having come from A grade bands, and most were virtuosos. Before I joined, they said they were a social band, but it's not true. To put salt in the wound, before the contest there was a lot of talk about them going to take part in the Provincial Contest. I was determined these blowhards were not going to take the cup away from my friends in Haversham and taint my grandfather's legacy, so I made a plan to sabotage their every attempt at winning it.'

'Ah—so we can stop here for a moment, and if I read out a list of the alleged misdemeanours, can you say yes to each of them if you are guilty of carrying them out?'

'I suppose so—I want to get this over and done with.'

Ann read out the list slowly while Isaac took notes, although he recorded the interview. When she had finished, she looked him in the eye and asked, 'Tell us why you decided to confess?'

Victor's eyes glazed over. He cleared his throat and said with a raspy voice, 'It's Grace—Grace and my daughter, Jill. When Grace asked you to tell me it's time to come home—I couldn't take it. Something went thud in my soul, and for the first time, I saw myself as I really am. I could see how much I'd neglected my family just for the sake of a bunch of cronies in a brass band, including me. I had put the cart before the horse and my loved ones missed out horribly. I also realised that my obsession had made me crazy and lost all sense of perspective. I went to such lengths to destroy a band's chances of winning a contest.' He had begun to stammer and sat forward with his face in his hands. When he lifted his face, it had turned red as he blinked away tears of remorse.

'I'm so sorry for all the trouble I've caused and the people I've hurt. I'll go to any length to put it right again—and if you don't lock me up, I will go back home and take care of my family,' he said snivelling and blowing his nose loudly into a not-so-clean handkerchief he hauled out of his pocket. 'You're not going to lock me up, are you?'

Ann glanced at Isaac and back at him again.

'It depends whether the victims of Riverlea Brassholes wish to lay charges. We are going to have to address each person, one by one to see. If none of them presses charges, perhaps we can let you go. But we'll hold you here until then.'

'So how long will that be and how many people will you need to talk to?'

Isaac nodded at Ann. She opened her dossier and removed a document.

'There's poor Will who had his backside severely burnt by the ammonia you spread on the toilet seat. Then there was Winnie who had to replace four expensive tyres on her Ute. The band had to pay out for their copier machine to get repaired. Apart from your pranks such as glueing drum cymbals together and wrecking a drum—worst of all, you disabled the podium causing Andre to break an arm. You could face a charge for grievous bodily harm.'

'But I didn't intend him to break anything—just to topple off the platform. I didn't think the whole thing would collapse like that as the screws were just loose, not removed.'

Isaac browsed at his notes which were a copy of those Ann had read out. 'Stealing Matt's keys is a punishable offence too.'

'I didn't steal them—I just borrowed them and put them back.'

Isaac shook his head in frustration.

'When I visited you with the spanner set, you said you didn't have a set like that. But you didn't admit you had a small spanner from that set. The rest of the tools you left with your son, who lives in Queenstown,' said Ann.

'When you asked me that day, I told the truth. I didn't have it as Jim kept hold of it after he retrieved it from the copier in case somebody claimed it.'

Mmm, he appears to have all the answers, thought Ann. But he could easily justify most of the demeanours as prankish behaviour unless a band member lays a charge.

'I think we should wind this up until we visit the band members concerned. We'll need the rest of the day to sort it to make sure no one wishes to prosecute.'

'What—are you going to keep me locked up all day?'

'No, we are not going to hold you, but you will hear from the court if anyone wishes to lay a charge.'

'What are you saying—I can go?'

Ann flashed Isaac a glance, and he nodded.

'Just for now, until I get in touch—don't leave town. You have caused your band a great deal of duress, and we must make sure they aren't taking it further.'

'It's not my band. Haversham Hooters will always be mine, but right now, I'm thinking of giving it up banding altogether. I'm going back home once you people release me to take care of my family like I should have done in the first place.'

'I'd like a word with my colleague, Victor. I'll turn off the recording, and we'll leave the room for a few minutes,' said Ann.

In another room, the two detectives discussed the options of employing the precepts of restorative justice, whereby Victor would meet with all of those concerned whom he had harmed or harassed and discuss ways of repairing the damage he had done to individuals and the band as a whole. After their discussion, they explained the process to him.

'I'll arrange with Andre to meet in the band room with everyone instead of the usual Wednesday practice. You can tell them everything you have told us today and seek their pardon, or forgiveness if you like. Ask them how you can make up for what you have done.' Ann watched his face, observing that it seemed to brighten at the prospect of being set free from the burden of guilt he had been carrying around.

Chapter Thirty-four

Ann and Isaac had sat through the meeting with Victor and the band members who appeared to have a sympathetic air about them after Victor had told his story, although he didn't sound self-pitying, which Ann thought had made the difference.

Even Will who had been burnt by the chemical attack was prepared to let it go. Andre, who'd sustained a broken arm which was still in a plaster cast only hoped he wasn't going to lose a good euphonium player and appeared upset that Victor was leaving town to live in Cambridge.

The committee asked to speak to the band alone after the meeting while Isaac and Ann took Victor into Andre's office.

After a good half hour of being shut in the room, it surprised Ann to see Martha rapping on the door, and to her delight, she was the sower of good news.

'What is it—what's the verdict?' Ann asked Martha, shaking with eagerness to get a result.

'They are unanimous in letting it all go—as long as you don't cause any further grief, Victor and promise to make a real go of it when you reunite with your family.'

'I don't know how to thank you all. I'm so sorry for all the mayhem I caused.'

Isaac turned to him,' On that, note—excuse the pun—Detective Grieves and I are closing your case, and you are now free to go.'

Victor was lost for words fighting back the tears of relief as the detectives walked towards the gathering of players with Victor shuffling behind. Ann's heart melted when various ones, including Will and Winnie, approached him, offering hugs.

'Come on,' Isaac said quietly to Ann tugging at her sleeve. 'I think our work is done here with this one. Now to follow up Johnny and see how he is going to squirm out of the mess he is in. Let's go.'

Ann let Martha know she would see her at home. Isaac dropped her off at her gate, but before she walked up the path to the house, she paused.

'What's the latest about Johnny?'

'His hearing is in two days. I meant to tell you his lawyer was able to procure a psychiatric report that will prove he has suffered post-traumatic-stress from the intimidation and bullying of the loan shark who threatened to harm his mother. I have the details of the swine, but we need to track him down. Perhaps you can come to the station tomorrow and help me do some work on finding him.'

'Sure, of course. Are you coming in for a coffee?'

'No, I've got a report to write up for today and another pile of paperwork. I'll see you at my office around nine tomorrow if that suits.'

After Isaac drove off, Ann got into her car and drove down to the village to the local Chinese Takeaway. She ordered a variety of food and took it home to surprise Martha, so she didn't have to worry about cooking. As she entered the driveway, Martha was just going in through the front door.

'Good timing,' said Ann. 'Dinner's up,' she said with a warm smile. I'd love some cold cider with this,' she said, holding up the meals in front of her. 'I want to hear all about your visit with Tom yesterday. We haven't had time for a catch-up yet.'

The women first reviewed the conclusion of Victor's enquiry into his confessed misdemeanours until Martha was eager to get onto the subject of Tom and Johnny.

'Alright then—spit it out,' said Ann, winking at Martha. 'I know you're bursting to tell me your news.'

Martha talked at length about how distressed Tom was the first time she visited him earlier in the week after Johnny's arrest.

'It broke my heart to see tears streaming down his face. I guessed he blames himself that he hadn't noticed what a state Johnny had got into in his cottage. He hadn't seen him in weeks.'

'How did he go this week when he visited him in custody?'

'He said Johnny was so remorseful and ashamed of putting his grandfather and mother through all the stress. He just couldn't cope when the loan shark said he would harm his mother. I guess he lost it.'

'Well, I know there's a good chance of the court granting him leniency because of mitigating circumstances. Just pray that he'll get a non-custodial sentence which he could likely get with a convincing psychiatric report.'

'I hope so. I don't think Tom would survive seeing his grandson incarcerated. That's why I said I would … um … I would support him.'

Ann searched Martha's face to read the unspoken words. She had got to know her friend very well.

'Mmm—what else do you want to tell me? You said when you walked in that you have some news for me.'

Martha coughed and cleared her throat.

'Tom kind of propositioned me or put me on the spot.'

'What—you mean he made a pass at you?'

Martha laughed loudly. 'Oh no, not that. He is the perfect gentleman. He asked if I would consider moving in for as long as I liked to assist with the house-keeping and help look after Johnny if he gets a non-custodial sentence—just until the lad sorts himself out.'

'Really? How do you feel about that?'

'To be honest—at first, I thought he was going to propose to me.'

'Is that what you were hoping? I didn't think you'd be interested in remarrying after Frank.'

'No, I wasn't hoping he'd ask that. I haven't even given marriage a thought. But I could see he needed support.'

'What did you say to him?'

'I said I needed time to think about it and to wait to see the outcome of Johnny's court hearing and I'll decide after that.'

'Well, you've got a lot to consider. Let's hope Johnny will get a decent judge and a favourable outcome.'

♫ ♫ ♫

Ann spent most of the next day with Isaac preparing the documents for Johnny's court case. According to the psychiatrist, he had a good chance of the judge showing him leniency and Tom had agreed to give evidence in his defence.

That evening, just as she was about to sit down and relax, Ann received a phone call from Victor.

'I received a letter from the police department saying no charges have been laid and I am free to leave town. I'm putting my house on the market tomorrow and leaving for Cambridge, but before that, I want to say I owe it to you for bringing my wife, daughter and me together. You persisted in getting me to own up to my misdeeds and put things right.'

'Thank you, Victor, but you also have Martha to thank for this. I couldn't have done it without her keen eye for detail and observation. When are you leaving? I hope you say goodbye to her too.'

'I'm leaving tomorrow after I've been with the Real Estate Agent. I suppose I'm too embarrassed to face her, but please tell her I'll be in touch, and I expect you both to come down and visit me in Cambridge.'

After he hung up the phone, Ann's heart somersaulted—a jump for joy.

Chapter Thirty-five

The hearing took all morning with a long break at midday. Johnny's mother, whom Isaac had interviewed after Johnny's confession, was sitting in the courtroom with the appearance of a black widow with Tom seated next to her, clutching her hand.

Ruth was persistent and forthright in her defence of Johnny as she read out the psychiatric report and gave full evidence of all mitigating circumstances.

As the judge finally summed up the court proceedings, Ann thought the tables were about to turn on poor Johnny, and he would receive a prison sentence. But as though by some miracle, the tide changed, and the judge imposed a suspended sentence on him with community detention for one year. He must reside on his grandfather Tom's property under supervision while continuing his university studies by distance learning. He must also check in with his grandfather each morning before working in the orchard and would be electronically monitored. The court will allocate him a Probation Officer.

While the judge pontificated on the restorative action Johnny would take towards Chad's family, his mother broke down sobbing. The apparent relief of her son being granted a non-custodial sentence overwhelmed her. Tom placed his arm around her as she sat quietly snivelling.

After the court was dismissed and the case closed, Ruth went over the court documents that stated how Johnny was to provide reparation to Chad's relatives by way of a letter seeking forgiveness. A payment settlement would be deducted from wages he earned in the orchard once it was up and running again. He also had a hefty fine to pay which Tom took care of and made it clear to him he would need to pay it back through his orchard work.

When Ruth had finished with him, and he met his Probation Officer, Johnny went home with Tom and his mother, who had come to stay with them for a few days.

Isaac waited while Ann buckled her seatbelt in his vehicle. 'Our job is done—as far as I can see. Johnny has plenty of reparation work to do, but I think we did well by him and Victor. You're a smart detective, Ann and I'm sure your old unit down south would have found it a great loss when you left.'

Ann smiled. 'Aw, thanks, Isaac.'

That made her day, but she'd had her years of sleepless nights out on the streets looking at dead bodies. Perhaps it was time for her to throw the towel in and stick to sorting out dysfunctional marriages and unfaithful spouses. One thing was sure—she was more eager than ever to take Scout and get back to her cottage by the sea and walks along the boulevard with her canine companion each morning. But first, she had to see that her best friend, Martha, would be alright, and she'd best get home to her now to catch her up on all the news. When Isaac dropped her off at Martha's gate, her heartstrings twanged when she thought this would likely be her last association with Isaac who had been a reliable and hardworking colleague.

'Are you sure you wouldn't like another job with the force?' he asked, winking with a warm smile.

'Ah, good try. Thanks again for inviting me to be on both cases. I didn't think I would be involved with a homicide enquiry again. Perhaps I'm not quite ready to be put out to pasture.'

'It would be an honour to have you help us out at any time. I'll still be in touch if I get stuck, as you told me, so don't enjoy the pasture too much,' he said as they both laughed.

'Bye for now,' he said, as he wound his window up and drove off.

♫ ♫ ♫

Ann would miss her friend and all the meals and loving care she'd lavished on her during her lengthy stay. She almost felt guilty about getting ready to pack up and leave and mulled over in her mind how she was going to tell her friend it was nearly time for her to return to her own home.

'I'm dying to hear all the news, but I've run you a hot bath first, and dinner is almost ready. I thought we'd have it early and then watch a chick flick to unwind.'

'You've got to stop spoiling me. It's going to be too difficult for me to go home and do it all myself.'

Ann almost fell asleep in the bath. She began thinking of Victor down in Cambridge and hoped she would soon hear how he was faring. Her sensitive nature was the reason she used to sob when she attended a homicide or suicide, as she always thought of the loved ones they left behind and cried for them. That's why her colleagues gave her the name of Calamity Ann instead of Ann Grieves, as they couldn't have a cop who was in a perpetual state of grief. She chuckled as she pondered her past role in the force.

There was a gentle tap on the bathroom door.

'Are you okay in there? I can keep your food in the warmer if you aren't quite ready,' said Martha, outside the door.

'Oh, sorry—I'm coming out now. Give me a few minutes.'

The warm bath had made Ann sleepy, and she could easily have crawled into bed without a meal—a direct result of too much adrenaline racing around in her body all week. But she had plenty to talk to Martha about and had to force herself to stay awake for a little longer.

While they both enjoyed Martha's lamb hotpot, one of her all-time favourite recipes and her finest batch of home-brewed ginger beer, Ann detailed the favourable outcome of Johnny's court case and sentence. Quite expectedly, Martha burst into tears, as she and Tom had been good friends since her Frank had passed away and she couldn't bear to think of his only grandson being locked up in prison.

'Thank God, our prayers have been answered. He was so distraught when I visited him the other day. He has been more than kind and generous to Johnny—he deserves a break.'

'So does his mother, by the look of her. She looked frazzled.'

'Tom said that once Johnny settles back on the orchard, Harriet will leave them both to it. She thinks her father can handle him far better than she can, and he needs a male role model. Tom is going to get Johnny to run the business, which will help him stay out of trouble.'

'What will his mother do? I don't know much about her,' said Ann.

'When Johnny was at University in Wellington, she moved down and bought herself a home there where she could work as a nurse. Recently she put it on the market and plans to move to Riverlea to be closer to her father and son, but she told Tom she wants her own space and doesn't want to interfere in his management of Johnny. She has found a job with a nursing agency where she can work anywhere. Her father had told her that Johnny was a man and didn't need to hang on to his mother's apron strings any longer.'

Ann dished up another bowl of hotpot and poured them both a drink.

'This lamb sure is tasty. I'm going to miss your cooking ... you do realise I'll have to leave soon.'

Martha cleared her throat and gulped her drink noisily. 'That's what I was getting to. Remember the other day I told you Tom had asked if I'd move in as housekeeper to help while he is supervising Johnny? Well—he asked me again if I would consider being his live-in companion and then he added housekeeper afterwards.'

'Ahem! What did he mean by that?' Ann winked. 'I hope he didn't intend hanky-panky.'

'Oh, no! He meant nothing like that—I've known him for years, and he's always been a gentleman and never made a pass at me. But I gather he's lonely and now he is feeling heavily disappointed and needs cheering up.'

'Is this what you want to do? What about your own home?'

'We discussed that, and he suggested I could rent it out, which I think is a great idea.'

'But what about all your animals? I don't think many tenants would want to take care of them.'

'That's just the point—they are coming with me too. Tom said he needs a goat to eat all the weeds growing between the fruit trees and there's plenty of ground that is fenced off. My hens and goose can run around with his, and he has a pig that would be an ideal mate for Hyacinth.'

'Goodness—it sounds as though you have it all sewn up—that didn't take long. But I understand you've been lonely since Frank died and you also deserve to be happy. I'm all for it.'

'So—how long before you depart from here?' Martha asked.

Ann looked searchingly in her friend's face and could see disappointment forming, but she knew that would be short-lived once she moved into Tom's farmhouse and began fussing over him the way she'd doted on her.

'How about a week? That'll give us time to tie up loose ends at the band room and for me to say goodbye to everyone.'

'I suppose that's alright—long enough for me to adjust to you leaving us. Let's leave the dishes until the morning and watch that movie we discussed earlier,' said Martha, preferring to focus on a more positive note.

'I've got an idea—why don't you invite Harriet around for a coffee tomorrow before she goes back to Wellington. That way, you can get to know her a bit better before you move in with Tom. Ask her for lunch, and I'll prepare something special.'

Martha's face lit up. 'Really—that's kind of you. Alright, I'll phone Tom's house and speak to her this evening.'

Chapter Thirty-six

Farewell Fair Maiden!

A week later

Ann was sad to leave Riverlea and the excitement of the chase. She and Martha were getting ready for her last practice with Riverlea Brassholes, and she would have to return her band uniform and the instrument they loaned her. They'd told her she could always come back and play any time and it was comforting to know that was still an option.

Things had moved fast in that neck of the woods since Johnny's court case, and he was beginning to settle back at the orchard with his grandfather. Martha was already busy planning her move into Tom's home.

'Breakfast is almost ready, Martha,' Ann said, calling to her from the back doorstep as she was hanging out her washing. 'Soon as you've finished with your laundry, make the most of my culinary skills while you can,' said Ann, chuckling and returning to the kitchen.

The landline rang. Ann scurried into the lounge to answer it just as Martha stepped back inside.

'It's Tom for you.'

Martha took the phone and wandered onto the veranda to talk to him. After she finished the call, Ann waited in the lounge with bated breath to hear an update about Tom. Snooping in doorways—a trait she'd developed after years of detective work.

'Good news—Tom said Harriet received a good offer on her home and has accepted it. Now she's panicking, as she'll soon have nowhere to live and I told him to let her know I'd help her find something here in the village.'

'But you have the perfect place for her—right here! Why don't you ask her if she would like to housesit until she finds a property she'd like to buy? That way, if it doesn't work out with Tom, you'll still have your home for the time being. It will give her time to look for a house and you the opportunity to see if you're going to be happy sharing a home with Tom.'

'Great suggestion! I'll phone Tom back and see what he thinks. This place is getting too much for me to look after. If it doesn't all work out, I'll still have to find a smaller home for myself.'

'We'd better get on. I need to take Scout for a walk after breakfast before we head off to practice, and I have a few phone calls to make.'

They sat down to Ann's speciality—Martha's home-grown blueberries and French Toast with cream which Martha had grown fond of and would miss once Ann was gone.

♫ ♫ ♫

Martha finished feeding all the animals just in time as Ann walked through the door with Scout.

'I need to get to the band room a little earlier today as the players are handing in all their music from the contest. Don't worry about lunch—I've packed a few sandwiches for us in my music satchel,' said Martha, as she scurried back and forth from her music room carrying her band gear into the lounge. 'By the way, there's a letter here addressed to both of us from Victor. It'll warm your heart.'

'Oh? Let's have a look,' said Ann, while Martha finished getting ready to go out.

The letter was a thank you note for pursuing the truth behind his emotional breakdown.

Dear Ann and Martha

This is a quick note to say how grateful I am (and so are my family) for pursuing the truth, no matter how ugly it appeared on the outside. You were both able to read between the lines, and you bravely spoke to the band about my difficulties and brought about healing in my family life. If it weren't for you two, I could have been arrested for grievous bodily harm to the players I injured.

♫ ♫ ♫

'Wow! I didn't expect so many people to be at practice so soon after the trouble they've had. The car park's full!' exclaimed Ann, driving slowly through the gate. 'I'll drop you off here with all our gear and then park down the back behind the trees.'

Martha thanked her and stumbled out while Ann drove off to find a space in the overcrowded parking area.

She was aware that Martha had wanted to arrive at the band room early and thought she'd go in and give her a hand to sort music before they started.

As she opened the door, she looked aghast at the hall full of coloured streamers and trestle tables covered with food. Someone was on the piano playing *For She Is A Jolly Good Fellow* while the band members sang the tune smiling at Ann.

That started her off—the floodgates opened as their gratitude overwhelmed her. Andre stood up and spoke after they'd finished their rousing welcome.

'Well, we all know how much we've enjoyed having you bail us out several times during the past month or so, and this is how we want to show our gratitude. We are sorry to lose you as a player, and the door is open any time you feel like coming for a blow. Just next time—leave your detective's hat behind,' he said, as they all laughed. 'We heard through the grapevine that Victor is doing well—and I guess we should be hoping the same for Johnny, although that one is a bit hard to swallow. I'm sure that in time we can forgive and forget.' On that note, Winnie came forward with a large bouquet and kissed Ann on the cheek while everyone clapped.

'Hey, how about my kiss?' called one of the players.

'And mine,' called another. The men continued the banter while they indulged in the food donated by the band committee.

'Oh, I forgot to say that this will be a short practice,' said Andre. 'It will be good to have a relaxed social time for a change—aside from dead bodies and burnt backsides.'

Chapter thirty-seven

'Goodness—time has flown since you first arrived. I can't believe you've almost been here for two months,' said Martha gloomily. 'I thought it would only be for a few days or at most, a week.'

'That's what you call being thorough. I couldn't go home knowing an axe-murderer was lurking in your neighbourhood, could I?' Ann replied winking at her friend who screwed up her face and shuddered. 'It could have been a right psychopath for all we knew at that stage, and I would not leave you in the lurch as friend or detective.'

'Oh, don't remind me. I'm trying to forget it all. Anyway—thanks to you we've discovered it was just poor Johnny, and I'd say he was in general, pretty harmless most of the time,' said Martha, wringing her fingers.

'So—when is D-day? You don't have to rush, you know.'

'I'm planning on heading home on Friday if that's okay. I have a client who has contacted me with a mystery she needs help solving. A family member has gone missing. I can't break her confidentiality, but it seems her mother is living with her and her husband, and she has been missing for twenty-four hours. She said that her husband wasn't getting on with her so looks like this could be a tricky one. For some reason, she won't call the police.'

Martha took their teacups out to the kitchen and came back to the dining table where they were sitting. 'Gracious—you're on a fresh case already! I thought you would take it easy and cut back.'

Ann grinned. 'It's like a magnet that draws you in—the hunt and the conquest. People like you and that woman often contact private detectives because they are protecting someone—a loved one, or in your case, your band, and want the investigation to be undercover. I guess it's something that my father passed on, and he was up to the mark.'

'So, what about your relaxed strolls with Scout along your boulevard? Perhaps that was just wishful thinking.' asked Martha with a half-smile.'

'Scout and I are a team. In a lot of cases, he helps me track and trace missing people. But of course, I didn't need him for the band crimes. I'll find him plenty of work to do that we can enjoy together, no problem there. And there'll be plenty of opportunities for strolling along the boulevard.'

Martha shook her head in disbelief.

'When are you making a move to Tom's place? You'll be lonely here when I go,' said Ann.

'I'll move in on the weekend after you've gone. By the way—I forgot to tell you Tom said that Harriet loved my house so much when she came for coffee that day that she would be keen to buy it if I'm interested in selling and gave me her phone number. I rang and asked if she would like to house sit until she finds something suitable, and the offer thrilled her.'

'What a great idea,' said Ann.

'I said I could leave it furnished which suited her, as Johnny requires household items which she could now offer him. I think she is happy to know her father will have a live-in house-keeper and companion, which lets her off the hook while she is working, not having to worry about him.'

'That's grand news. Don't fret, Martha—it'll work out. God is good and has brought a favourable outcome from tragic circumstances already. You'll be just fine, and if not, you get to keep your house, and perhaps I can come and stay with you from time to time.'

Ann detected a touch of sadness on Martha's face. 'Everything alright?' she asked.

'It's just the animals I'm considering. I know I can take them all with me to Tom's, but what about the budding friendship between Hyacinth and Scout? I mean—already Hyacinth shares the dog kennel with him during the day, and they seem inseparable out in the orchard. Hyacinth will miss him terribly.'

Ann went quiet briefly. 'Of course—but what about Tom's pig you told me about? He sounds friendly.'

'Oh, that's Hercule—Hercule Poirot. He gets that name from sniffing around everywhere. I guess he will welcome her.'

Ann knew her friend was only projecting her insecurity of leaving the home she'd lived in for thirty years of her married life. Still, she knew that once Martha started running around after Tom and Johnny, she wouldn't have time to worry about the emotions of her animals. She was mirroring the loss she would feel when her best friend was about to leave.

'I tell you what. Let me know when your band is about to enter another contest next year, and I'll think about sitting in at your rehearsals and possibly giving it another whirl. There's still a bit of life left in this old girl yet. And who knows—once I retire, you may even see me back in uniform and a confirmed member of the Riverlea Brassholes Band.'

With that last statement, Detective Ann Grieves got up and walked off to her room to pack ready for the next calamity—another Cosy Mystery to solve.

♫ ♫ ♫ The End ♫ ♫ ♫

Author Bio

Patricia, known as Trish, grew up in a small town in New Zealand. From the age of five, she rode horses which her family-owned and trained, often winning prizes in the local horse shows. During her early life, her parents lived off the land, initially share-milking and later as horticulturists.

After completing her nursing studies and qualifying as a Registered Nurse, Patricia spent six years abroad, living in Australia and Europe doing a variety of jobs between her nursing roles. She returned to Auckland to start a family and currently enjoys her role as a doting grandmother.

After a forty-year nursing career, Patricia retired and now writes inspirational Cosy Mysteries and Romantic Suspense set in beautiful New Zealand.

Patricia writes a New Zealand brand fiction portraying the spectacular local scenery, wildlife and Kiwi culture. She gains her ideas from her own experiences and the vast amount of travelling she has done in NZ and overseas.

VISIT ME:

patriciasnelling.com

https://www.facebook.com/PatriciaSnellingAuthor/

https://www.instagram.com/patriciasnellingnovels/

I would love to receive an honest review if you wish to leave one on any online website or your blog. Thank you!